MW01242095

Stranded in the Everglades

A Mitchell Lavender Series Book Two

S. Willett

S. Willett
5816 N. Bailey
Coral, Michigan 49322
www.swillett.com

Publisher's Note: This is a work of fiction. Names, characters, places, and incidents are a product of the author's imagination. Locales and public names are sometimes used for atmospheric purposes. Any resemblance to actual people, living or dead, or to businesses, companies, events, institutions, or locales is completely coincidental.

Cover Artist – Lisa Messegee – www.thewritedesigner.com
Book Layout © 2017 BookDesignTemplates.com

Stranded in the Everglades. -- 1st ed.
ISBN 9798723456266

Thank you to a traveler of the USA and good friend, **Lois Krieger**, and my faithful editor and long-time friend, **Susan Davis.**

Contents

CHAPTER ONE

My Trip

My morning started like any other school day until I came down for breakfast and found Dad still home. I glanced out of the kitchen window and saw a fresh layer on the snow-covered ground, but it didn't appear to be so deep to call off school or stop my dad from going to work. An unwelcomed chill ran through my bones when I heard the wheezing.

My parents sat at the table in the breakfast nook. "What's up?" I asked, hoping for the best. But Mom, still in her pajamas, and Dad, dressed for work, had pulled his chair next to her. The way she sat with her spine straight and her head tilted back slightly to help her breathe, told me the whole story.

"Mitchell, I'm taking your mom to the hospital to get checked over. She's having trouble breathing again. Get your breakfast and go to school. We'll see you this afternoon."

I walked to the sink and stared out of the window. How could she be sick? She's only like forty-something. That's way too young to be seriously ill. I turned to face her when she cleared her throat to speak.

"Don't worry, honey, they'll probably give me another breathing treatment and orders to see my doctor. When you get home from school, we'll go over our trip to the Everglades. It's just a few days away."

Dad grabbed Mom's coat from the hall closet and helped her into it. Seconds later, they were on their way.

Mom always played her breathing problems as no big deal, but I worried. It had become a regular event. I thought about staying home but today was the last day before Christmas break.

The day dragged but being a reporter for the school newspaper made everyday fun. Last fall, I had written a couple of articles that put me in the spotlight. The rodeo story turned out to be fun and my best writing ever. I learned a lot, gained several new friends, and found a very special girl, Haylee. I hoped to spend more time with her, but that might be unlikely. For some reason, she would not have anything to do with me. I know for certain that she liked me, and we shared a common love for animals.

When I got home from school, Dad had gone to work, and Mom sat at the table, fully dressed, gazing at her laptop. "The doctor, just like I told you, gave me a treatment. I'll be just fine. Everything is A-Okay."

I pulled out a chair and sat close enough to see the computer screen. "That's good. You look better, and there isn't as much wheezing."

"Mitchell, we will be staying in Miami near the shopping district. There are several unique places to eat and shop. Look at the rooms in this house." Mom pointed at the computer screen.

I glanced at the rooms pictured, swallowed hard, and shook my head. Shouldn't mothers automatically know that guys my age want adventure? This trip, my trip, to the Florida Everglades didn't appear to be on the right track, and I didn't know how to control the plan. I studied the open map next to me and tried not to be mouthy.

"Why did you book a place in Miami?" I pointed at the Everglades south of Miami and continued, "We need to be close to the Everglades, so I can take photos and do some research." I wanted to stay calm, but my next words spat out, "I don't care where we sleep."

"We'll rent a car and drive to the swamp every day. The place where we are staying is not that far from the Everglades, and in town, you'll be able to go to the museums and the zoo. I'm sure they will have interesting details about the Everglades at those places, too."

"Mom, I need to be able to smell, feel, and live that environment to be able to write a good article for *Earthly Creatures Magazine*. I want to see alligators in the wild, watch a snake slither through the grass, take a ride on an airboat, and see the mangroves. There's so much to discover." I wished Dad was going, but he had "important" stuff going on at work. He would understand that I needed to be close to the action.

She ignored me and said, "And the magazine's office is in Miami, so you'll be able to ask them questions if need be. Plus, I can't be that far from help should we need it. I wouldn't feel comfortable deep in that swamp."

I folded the map shut and said, "Mom, what kind of help would we need? Are you worried about your breathing? I thought you said everything is okay." I shouldn't have said that. The wheezing happened too often. Everything was not 'okay,' and I shouldn't have brought it up. The doctor had that job.

She shut her laptop and fidgeted with the cord. Mom seldom appeared unhinged, but that was what I saw now. Guilt washed over me. The words I had just said echoed in my head, but I waited for an answer.

Finally, she glanced up and said, "You never know what might happen in a place so far from home. That's just the way it's got to be." She picked up her computer and left the room.

"Mom, I'm going out to the Goodrich farm today. Is that all right with you? Andy will be here in a few minutes."

She answered with a short, "It's okay."

I took the stairs two at a time to my room. Glancing around, I found my boots under the desk next to a stack of books about the Everglades. I'd made my bed but sat on it anyway to pull my boots on, then ran downstairs. After grabbing my coat, I burst out of the door. Andy, the best bull rider ever, waited in his truck.

He never quit talking on the way to the farm. I half-listened but mostly thought about who might be there. I hoped Haylee. And you'll never guess the first person I saw as we drove up to the barn. *Haylee*.

She led the Bronco out of the barn. I shouldn't call that horse a bronco anymore. He trusted Haylee and me to put a halter on him, but the only one that could ride him was me. I earned his trust months ago.

Haylee was all bundled up with a coat, a knit hat, and leather gloves. She smiled at us then continued leading the horse to the corral.

Andy slammed the truck into park and hopped out. "Where is everyone?"

"No one is answering their phones. I don't even know where Landon is. The whole Goodrich family is gone. They'll be happy that I'm caring for the horses," Haylee said and glanced at the truck.

I could hear them, and it seemed weird just sitting in the truck staring. The sound of a horn alerted me to an approaching car.

Andy bellowed out, "Hey Mitchell, that's your dad's car."

Dad drove, and someone sat in the passenger seat. As they drew closer, I recognized that the other person was Mateo. Why would Dad have my friend with him? I stepped out of the truck. The snow crunched under my feet.

Mateo taught me how to rope and ride like a cowboy. He seldom smiled but, right now, he had a smile that shone over his whole face. He opened the door before the car came to a stop, jumped out, and ran toward me. At the same time, he announced, "We're going to the Everglades. You and me. We are going to the Everglades." He almost knocked us both to the ground with the force of his forward motion and squeezed me into a giant bear hug.

"What are you talking about?" I couldn't comprehend the words he'd said.

"Your dad asked me to go with you to Florida. Just you and me. We're going to the Everglades." It didn't seem possible that the smile on his face got bigger, but it did.

I turned my attention to Dad. "Mateo and I are going to Florida by ourselves?" That sounded very cool, or did it?

Dad laughed then said, "My boss has a brother, Steve, who lives in Homestead. He's going to meet you guys at the airport and let you stay at his house. Homestead is close to the Everglades. Your mom won't be happy about it. She thinks she's healthy enough to go, but I don't."

CHAPTER TWO

Change of Plan

Dad stood beside me near the corral and said, "I asked Mateo's dad before talking it over with you, but I knew you'd love the idea of going to Florida with a friend. There will be rules like calling me every day, but this will be good for you boys to be somewhat on your own. Steve is on disability, so he will have free time to show you around. He lives right in Homestead."

"Is Mom going to be okay?"

"She'll be mad, but you're fairly responsible, and you need this trip."

"I mean her health. Is there more going on than you're telling me?"

"I don't know how to answer that. No, we've told you everything. They did some tests and we'll soon find out more about these breathing issues." Dad put his hand on my shoulder. "We have to keep living life, which reminds me that I'd better go to work."

Mateo joined me as we watched my dad drive away. He still wore a smile and gave me a high-five. "Your dad came over this morning and talked with my family and me. When he asked my parents if I could go with you to Florida to help you with your research, I couldn't believe my luck, but I knew the answer would be no for two reasons. First, it's Christmas, and secondly, because we don't even know this guy Steve. After a long back and forth talk, they said yes. My heart has been on overdrive ever since."

"I'm as surprised as you are. I'm not sure how this will all play out, but it's sure to be an adventure." My excitement soared.

"Yeah, adventure. Florida. The Everglades. Just us against the wilderness." Mateo's eyes had a sparkle in them.

Surprised at his wording, I shot him a look. "Mind if I use your words in my article? I like the thought of us against the wilderness." *Little did I know that's exactly what our future would bring.*

He stared at the ground and kicked the dirt. When he looked up, a spark of mischievousness shone in his eyes. "We're gonna have a good time."

Haylee brought Molly out of the barn, heading to the corral. Molly whinnied when she saw me, or at least, that's what I'd like to think. I went inside the fence to help with the saddle and give some love to the Bronco. Haylee asked, "Have you been to the jail to see Greg yet?"

I shook my head. "No, I don't see any reason I should go. You do remember that he tried to kill me. Not once, but twice."

"He's a mixed-up kid. They're sending him to prison very soon. The county jail is bad, but prison will be awful for him."

Andy stood just outside the corral and said, "I heard he was sentenced ten to fifteen years in Jackson State Prison. Why would they be sending him to prison? I think he's only sixteen."

My jaw tensed, and I said, "Trying to kill someone is a pretty serious crime. He probably would be better off in a place that could rehab him. You know, help him see that he's not looking at things the right way."

"He's almost eighteen, and Mitchell's right; they tried him as an adult because of the seriousness of his crime. Prison probably isn't the best place for him." Haylee had an edge to her voice when she spoke to Andy, and then she turned to me using a softer tone. "But to get back to what I'm trying to tell you, Mitchell, I know that Greg wants to talk to you. I think he wants to apologize. You shouldn't deny him the right to confess to you what he did. Maybe you'll even find out why."

"You're so innocent." I stopped right there because the look on her face appeared far from innocent, and I'd seen her temper. So, I ended the conversation with, "I'll think about it." I stepped toward Andy. "Hey, can you give Mateo a ride home, too?"

"Sure. You guys ready?"

I turned to Haylee. "You want a hand getting on the horse?" Her face told me how stupid my question was, so I laughed and said, "Just kidding. I came out today to say goodbye to everyone. It seems Mateo is joining me on a trip to Florida for a week and a half."

Haylee walked over and hugged me. "We will all miss you guys. Please be careful. I think the Everglades are dangerous." She walked toward Molly, then turned and said, "Think about going to see Greg. It might be good for both of you."

I couldn't move for a minute. The hug surprised me. *Maybe she likes me more than even she knows.* Andy and Mateo got in the truck. I watched as Haylee rode off on Molly, wishing I was with her.

Andy hollered out of the window, "You got it bad for her. Come on, let's go."

The guys attempted to outdo each other with wild comments about my lack of a love life. I worked to keep a straight face.

Mateo went quiet and stared out the side window. Finally, he spoke. "Maybe we should go see Greg."

Mateo's words brought me back to reality. "You must be kidding?"

Andy said, "Haylee might be right about him wanting to get clear of what he tried to do. I don't know if you guys know it, but Greg's dad died in a car accident when he was young. His mom remarried two years after. The stepdad is a drunk, and Greg hates him. I don't think he ever got over losing his real dad."

"That truly is a sad story," I meant to keep the anger out of my wording. "But it doesn't excuse what he has done. I'm not sure what I'd have to say to him."

Mateo's eyes appeared sad, and he quickly glanced away. He didn't say anything.

I gave up the fight. Maybe they were right. "We're leaving on Sunday for Florida. If we're going to visit Greg, it will have to be tomorrow."

CHAPTER THREE

Jail

We pulled into the parking lot at the same time Haylee, with tissue to her face, walked out of the County building. Her shoulders drooped, and she stumbled.

After Andy parked, I jumped out and ran toward Haylee. I took her hand, and the crying intensified for a few minutes. She gripped my hand while her other held the tissue to her nose.

When Andy and Mateo joined us, she pulled her hand away, turning her attention toward them. "He's not here. They took him to Jackson. I can't drive that far, and I don't think his mom will either."

She choked back her anguish and forced out the words, "He'll be all alone."

My body stiffened. *Haylee loves Greg.* She started talking again, but I didn't want to hear.

"We've worked the rodeo together for years." She looked at Andy then Mateo. "Just like you guys, we're like family. He's like a brother to me."

Brotherly love. That's better.

"You can write letters to him. Just make sure he knows you love him like a brother." The minute the words left my mouth, I knew it was trouble.

"What?" Haylee's hands fisted on her hips. "What did you say?"

I took a step forward, knowing I'd have to own the statement I'd just made. "We all know he doesn't love you like a sister. It's deeper than that for him. You told me yourself that he scared you sometimes."

Haylee stared at the ground for a moment, then looked at us. "I knew him before his mom remarried. Her new husband hurt Greg over and over, turning him into someone that can hate. I can't just walk away."

"If you write him daily and go to see him, you are letting him think you feel the same way about him as he does you. I'm not saying you shouldn't write ever."

Andy, in a gentle tone, backed me up. "He'll only get worse in prison. Maybe Mitchell is right, Haylee."

"Maybe he is." She turned away from us, got in her car, and drove away without saying goodbye. I wouldn't see her for at least two weeks.

"No sense in standing around here," Andy said.

Mateo asked, "Well, what are you doing?" He shook me by the shoulder. "Mitchell, you okay?"

"Yes, deep thoughts. That's all. I should go home, make sure everything is all ready, and spend some family time. We leave early tomorrow."

Mateo grinned. "I washed and packed my clothes last night. What kind of stuff are you taking?"

Andy kicked at a stone on the cement then stared at Mateo. "Why did Mr. Lavender pick you, Mateo, and not me?"

Andy had hurt feelings. I also wondered why my dad picked Mateo. I spend more time with Andy. I had to say something to help fix the damage. "Really. What was he thinking?"

Everyone was silent for a minute, then Andy burst out laughing and we joined him.

After the laughter died down, and Mateo had made a few wisecracks, he asked, "Are you bringing a pocket knife?"

"I don't have a knife."

"Didn't think so. I'll bring mine."

"You never know, we might need a knife. You know that you can't carry it on the plane, right? You'll have to pack it."

Andy pulled into the driveway, and I got out. "Andy, while we're gone, keep an eye on Haylee. See you early tomorrow, Mateo."

****

Christmas music boomed from the Google speaker, and Mom hung another bulb on the tree.

"Hey, I thought we weren't going to decorate this year." I took a look from every angle at what she'd done so far. Mom could trim a tree, and she knew I loved it.

"Your dad didn't want us to go to the trouble, but I'll be home. Will you help me?"

"Sure, I'll help. Where's Dad?"

"He's in his office, exchanging my name on the airline ticket to Mateo's. He's been in there quite a while. Did you see Greg Wilkerson?"

The lights were already on the tree, so I donned the icicles. "No, when we got there, Haylee told us they had taken Greg to Jackson yesterday."

"Haylee was there?" Mom stopped halfway up the ladder and made a slight turn toward me.

"We talked about her going to see him. She feels guilty about him being all alone. The guys and I warned her about leading him on."

"I hope you didn't use those words."

Nervous laughter spilled out. "You know Haylee pretty good. I didn't say it quite like that."

"I saw his mom yesterday afternoon. Of course, she's very upset. I guess Greg's stepdad is not a very nice person. Let's change the subject. Are you all packed? Dad is taking us out to dinner tonight."

"I have to pack my carry-on, but the suitcase is all ready to go."

Mom, Dad, and I spent the rest of the afternoon putting up decorations, singing along with the Christmas carols, and talking about holiday memories. Dad took us to a very nice restaurant, and Mom never once acted like she was upset about not going. She hardly mentioned Florida at all.

Mom had made me a list of things I would need, so I double-checked the suitcase and packed the carry-on. I brought my suitcase downstairs and put it in the trunk of the car. The house was dark except for the tree.

Something about the Christmas tree lights radiated a sort of comfort, so I grabbed a couch pillow and laid on the floor, gazing up at it. I worried about my mom, but doctors can heal most anything. My mind turned to the Everglades. I couldn't believe Mateo and I were making this trip by ourselves.

Then I wondered about Steve in Homestead and what kind of guy he might be. The town was only about ten miles from the Everglades with tours and airboat rides. The airboat rides were expensive. Dad gave me some Traveler's Checks to help with the trip, but most of the money I planned to take was what I had earned.

I must have dozed off because I awoke to a hurting back from sleeping on the floor. I half sat up and glanced at the window to see complete darkness, then startled at a noise from the kitchen.

Mom pulled the step stool over to a kitchen cupboard and reached up to get the syrup. Breakfast. She was already making breakfast.

Florida

Then it hit me. Today was the day I would be going to Florida. I threw off the blanket and bounded into the kitchen to hug Mom. Her red-rimmed eyes said one thing, but the smile spoke something else.

"Why have you been crying?" I knew she had wanted to go on this trip. My cheeks grew hot with some kind of weird guilt.

"You know I would have loved going to Florida with you, but I have to be here for the follow-up with the doctor. This breathing thing has gone on for too long. We have to get to the bottom of it and find out why."

Dad, fully dressed, came up behind me and took me by both shoulders. "Good morning. It's going to be quiet here, without you. It would have been a sad Christmas without both of you. I'm glad you're staying here with me, Sandy." Leave it to Dad to smooth things over.

"That's not what you said before." Mom smiled and glanced at the dining room. "Go sit at the table, both of you."

"Just a minute, I forgot to bring in the mail yesterday, and there was a letter from *Earthly Creatures* for Mitchell. I'll be right back." Dad threw on his coat, stepped into the garage, and returned in only a few minutes.

I couldn't sit. I'd sent an article to the magazine about a month ago. I'd made friends with the magazine's editor, and he suggested that I submit my story about the rodeo. He also thought I should write about the Everglades. Thank goodness that Dad didn't take long bringing in the mail. I ripped open the envelope and read the bad news.

Mom scrunched her eyebrows, making her forehead wrinkly, and stepped closer. "What did they say?"

"They rejected the rodeo article. Blah, blah, they say, in so many lovely ways, to try again." I threw the open letter on the table for them to read. "There's no need to go to Florida. My writing is not good enough for a real magazine. I should have known that."

Dad read the complete letter. His jawline tensed. "You are going to Florida." He turned to Mom. "Sandy, give Mitchell twenty minutes to get his shower and dress before putting breakfast on the table." "Mitchell, remember not to dress in Michigan clothes. It will be hot there."

Mom spoke out right away, "Roger, you're being insensitive. Can't you see the boy is hurting?"

Dad held his tongue for a minute. "He's not a kid anymore. Success often comes with pain. Let's not make him into a quitter."

Dad couldn't understand how I felt and wouldn't even try. Even so, I did what he had ordered. It didn't take long to get showered, back to the kitchen, and eat. After my goodbyes to Mom, we were on the road. I decided not to tell Mateo about the rejection letter. We would have fun on this trip, even if I didn't write the story. I'm glad Dad insisted on me making the trip.

Mateo and his whole family, even his Grandpa, were outside when we pulled into the driveway. You could tell they were all happy for him. Not that he was leaving, but that he had this chance for adventure.

Their joking about the two of us on our own served to lighten the mood between Dad and me, as well as give Mateo a happy send-off. Mateo leaned out of the window to wave, letting the cold air in and freezing us.

Dad gave us our instructions on the way to the airport. Check-in first, then go to the designated waiting area, stay safe, be smart, and don't forget to call every day. He didn't want to park the car and go in with us. Instead, he pulled up to the United Airlines sign, helped us unload the trunk, and we said our goodbyes.

"I don't want to leave your mom any longer than I have to. You boys will be fine. Call if something goes wrong." He hugged me and whispered, "I love you." He got in the car and drove away.

Watching him leave gave me a nervous pit in my stomach. Would we be fine? I'd never been on my own like this.

I turned to Mateo and knew he had a similar moment. Then we shared a grin, picked up our bags, and went into the bustling area of the building. We checked in with no problem and went right to the waiting area.

"I've never flown before. Have you?" Mateo sat across from me.

"First time for me too. Are you worried?"

"No, I just want the window seat. It's an adrenalin thing." He checked his watch. "We have an hour before boarding. I can't just sit here." Mateo rose to a stand. "Let's go find the gift shop."

After not finding anything to buy in the gift shop, we tried the restaurant. Even though both of us had eaten breakfast, we each gobbled down a large cinnamon roll and a mug of hot chocolate.

The announcement echoed through the building, "Boarding for United flight 307 to Miami."

After leaving a tip, we ran down the passageway to the waiting area and got in line to board the plane. The cold air swirled through the cracks in the ramp walkway. The stewardess and pilot greeted us, and we found our seats. Neither of us put our carry-on in the overhead storage.

A lady and her little boy of maybe six sat in front of us. The boy stood in the seat and stuck his tongue out at us before asking, "Where are you guys going?"

Mateo leaned forward toward the boy. "Miami, and then on to the Everglades. Where are you going?"

"We're going to Miami, too, to see my grandmom. Did you know there are snakes in the Everglades?"

"I get bucked off bulls. You think I'm afraid of a snake?" Mateo asked.

"You're a cowboy?"

Mateo just grinned while I took in the funny scene playing out in front of me.

"Well, even cowboys got to be scared of panthers. Did you know there are panthers in the Everglades?"

I pointed at Mateo and said, "He would take a rope, make a lasso, and tie up any old panther."

The little boy's eyes got big, and then his mom made him turn around and buckle up. We laughed and buckled, too. I pulled out my phone to make a note of the little kid and put my phone on airplane mode.

Mateo focused on the window, and the plane's take-off, then once in the air, he continually pointed out ground visuals and cloud formations. I let him know that I should have the window seat on the way home. The short, smooth flight didn't even give me time to read. Instead, I studied the people around me.

The warm air and sun welcomed us to Miami as we walked across the tarmac after leaving the plane. The little boy ran up, pushed between Mateo and me, and held each of our hands. His mom laughed and pulled him closer to her. We entered the building and waved goodbye. I scanned the crowd for Steve, checking the picture I had of him on my phone.

We hit the restroom then got our luggage. Still no Steve, so I called him. No answer.

"Maybe he got held up in traffic. Miami is a big town," Mateo threw his bag over his shoulder, acting all confident, but something told me he was worried, too.

"I think we should go back to the waiting area where we disembarked. Steve would probably go there." We did and waited. I wondered if I should call my dad, but I didn't want him to worry. He had enough on his mind, so I sent a short text to let him know that we were in Florida.

After about an hour, we headed to the luggage area—no Steve. We had him paged. No Steve.

"I'm hungry, and right over there is a place we could eat." Mateo pointed at a large area in the center of the airport's lobby with tables set for dinner.

"Okay, the tables are out in the open. Steve would be able to see us, and we can keep an eye out for him while we eat."

"Hey, do you think there are panthers in the Everglades?"

I stopped and turned to face him, searching his face for fear, but all I saw were eyes filled with wonder. "Yes, for sure there are panthers, but they'd have a hard time getting to us. We'll be on an airboat."

We both ordered burgers, fries, and coleslaw. While we were eating, I saw Steve. "Be right back. Wait here." I did a fast walk.

The guy walked fast, so I picked up my pace to finally catch up. "Hey, I'm Mitchell. My friend, Mateo, is over there." I pointed to the dining area.

"Cool, let's get going." Steve didn't shake hands, explain why he was late, or show any normal reaction. He turned and walked away.

Mateo stood at the bar paying our bill. I ran back, grabbed my bags, and motioned. "Come on. We don't want to lose him."

Once in the car, I expected Steve to tell us what happened or talk about the Everglades. Nope, not one word in the forty-five-minute ride to Homestead. Mateo glanced my way every once in a while. I'm sure he was perplexed, too.

Steve pulled up to a small, rundown house and left the car running. We all got out, and he led us into the house.

"This is it. Not much, but it's free." Steve opened the door and stepped to the side to let us in.

We entered the living room portion of a large room with a kitchen at the far end. An open door revealed the bathroom, and two other closed doors, probably bedrooms.

"Thank you for picking us up, and thanks for letting us stay. Will we be going to the Everglades tomorrow?" I set my bag on the carpeted floor.

"Hold it right there, buddy. I'm not your babysitter or tour guide. My brother asked me to give you a place to stay. You won't see much of me. I'll take you back to the airport when it's time." With that, he walked out, leaving us with our mouths open and staring at the closed door.

CHAPTER FIVE

Boarded Windows

"Nothing has gone right since we landed in Florida," I glanced about the open kitchen/living room set up. "How are we ever going to get to the Everglades?"

"You said it was only ten miles. We can walk that far," Mateo opened one of the doors. "Hey, this must be Steve's bedroom. Wow, what a mess. The rest of the house is clean. I hope." He opened the other bedroom door.

That bedroom had two twin beds, a dresser, and a small desk. "Very clean and neat. I guess we'll take this room."

I chuckled because things could have been worse. Steve might not have shown up at all. Then where would we be?

The kitchen had a few dirty dishes, but the table was bare except for a set of keys probably for the house. Mateo opened the fridge. "A trip to the store is in order, but we planned on buying our groceries anyway. So, to sum it all up, we have a roof over our heads, money to buy groceries, and we can walk to the Everglades and take an airboat ride."

"You're right. We have it made. Let's take a look outside after we put our stuff in the bedroom." I shouldered my carry-on, picked up my suitcase, and headed for the bedroom.

It had gotten even warmer in the early afternoon sun. The front yard consisted of a tiny bit of yard and a cement sidewalk that led into town. In the backyard, we found an old truck and a newer motorboat on a trailer. Weeds had grown up around both.

Our search led us to a boat motor braced over a barrel of water positioned closer to the house. Mateo, about to pull the starter rope, jumped when a male voice surprised him.

"What are you boys doing?"

I spun around to see Steve, standing by the house with hands-on-hips.

Mateo didn't seem surprised to see Steve. "Just checkin' out the place. Does this motor work?"

"It used to. If you get bored and have the know-how, you have my permission to fix it, and then you'll be able to see the Everglades." Steve walked closer to us, and I noticed a Magic City Casino member card hanging on a lanyard around his neck. "I forgot to tell you that my bedroom is off-limits, but I see that you've already found your room." He handed me a slip of paper with a phone number. "Call, only if it's life or death." He went back into the house and then left without another word.

"We don't need to make a list for the store, do we?" Mateo asked.

"No, let's go." I headed in the opposite direction of town.

"What are we doing?"

"We have plenty of time, so I thought we'd get a lay of the land. You know, see what's all around us."

We hadn't gone far when Mateo pointed at an old lady boarding her windows. She struggled to lift a large square of plywood. We ran to help her.

"Oh, thank goodness. I'm so glad to see you." She took a closer look. "I've never seen either of you around here."

A glance at Mateo told me that, this time, I would be our speaker. "We just got here today from Michigan and took a round-about way to get groceries. This is Mateo, he's a rodeo cowboy, and my name is Mitchell. I'm a writer, and that's why we came. I want to write about the Everglades." I lifted the plywood into place, and Mateo pounded the nails.

Mateo stopped pounding and asked, "I thought the weather was going to be sun, sun, sun. Are we in for a storm?"

She nodded toward the next window and pointed at another piece of plywood. "I'm Violet and have lived in Homestead my whole life, almost eighty years. The weather guy says sun, sun, sun, but I know better. Can't you feel the storm brewing?" Violet pointed to the south.

"Feel it?" Mateo and I echoed, glancing up at a cloudless sky.

Violet laughed and shrugged her shoulders. "You're from Michigan. What would you know about storms?"

"We have storms." I took another piece of plywood from Violet.

"You will see." She shook her head. "The Everglades," Violet paused as if thinking, and then continued, "it's a place of sunshine and abundant animal, reptile, and aquatic life." She waited until we were both looking at her, and then she took a step closer and whispered, "But don't be fooled, there are dark places and secrets in the Everglades." She changed the subject. "Where are you staying?"

For a moment, neither of us answered. I couldn't get her words out of my head – *Dark places and secrets.* Mateo nudged me. "Uh, Steve. Um, Steve Fredricks' place just down the road."

"You're staying with Steve?" Violet dropped the piece of plywood she'd been holding.

"Sort of. He dropped us off at his house and said we wouldn't see much of him." I picked up the piece of plywood she had dropped. "You sound surprised. My mom was going to bring me, and we would have stayed in Miami, but she's not well. So, Dad set us up with Steve. Dad works with Steve's brother."

"So, your dad doesn't know Steve, does he?"

"No, Dad only knows his brother. Is he a bad guy?"

"Steve's all right, but you can't depend on him. How are you going to get to the Everglades?"

Mateo spoke up. "It's only ten miles. We can walk and then take one of those airboat rides." He pounded in the last of the nails.

Violet nodded and smiled. "That was our last window, so let's go in and get a cookie."

Her house seemed dark, but we had just boarded up her windows. She turned on a few lights, poured us each a glass of milk, and set a plate of chocolate chip cookies on the table.

We sat, and I took a cookie, soft yet crunchy around the outside. "Delicious."

Violet pushed the plate closer to us. "Don't be so polite, have a couple. Do you know about the super snakes?"

"There are snakes everywhere, but I'm sure your snakes are bigger." I knew quite a bit about the environment of Florida.

"So, you don't know about them. You need to know, and I will tell you." She took a chair. "Hurricane Andrew bore down on Florida in 1992 with sustaining winds of 150 mph that tore buildings apart. One building, in particular, bred Burmese pythons. Other exotic wildlife buildings also succumbed to the storm. Since then, the Burmese and Indian pythons have interbred. We now have what they are calling super snakes that can grow to twenty feet long and weigh two-hundred pounds."

I laughed because Mateo's Adam's apple danced up and down his throat when she said that. Violet must have misunderstood my laugh.

She continued, "You laugh, but to us here in Florida, it is serious. They have eaten most of the raccoons, rabbits, and foxes. They have been known to eat deer, our pets, and even people. I've heard that the super snakes are migrating north into Georgia."

Wide-eyed Mateo asked, "They said something about that at school. Have you ever seen a python?"

"Yes, several times." She picked up our glasses and put them in the sink. "Thank you for helping me today. Now, I will help you."

We both stood and followed her to the front door.

"After you get groceries, go back to Steve's, and I'll send someone that will take you to the Everglades later this afternoon. It will be a short trip because it's already afternoon, but I assure you it will be worthwhile."

CHAPTER SIX

Airboat

Shopping didn't take long, and then we hurried back to unload. Mateo carried three bags of groceries into the kitchen while I had two bags and a case of pop. We would eat like kings. I threw the refrigerated items into the fridge and had just started helping Mateo with the canned goods and snacks when we heard a knock on the door.

My phone chimed at the same time, so Mateo hurried to the door.

Haylee texted, asking if we were enjoying our vacation. I glanced up to see Mateo turn to face me with a wide-eyed, smiley face. I quickly texted

Haylee that nothing had gone as planned, and I'd text her later when I knew more. That wouldn't go over, but Mateo had me curious.

I stepped across the room. A girl, a few years older, reached out to shake my hand. I extended mine, stunned at her firm grip. "Hi."

"Like I told your friend, my name is Emmie. Grandma Violet sent me to take you on an airboat ride. Are you ready?"

No wonder Mateo couldn't talk. This pretty lady was the answer to any guys' dreams. Who would have thought that doing a good deed would turn out so perfect? I glanced beyond Emmie to see a truck with a trailered airboat.

She didn't wait for an answer but instead turned and walked toward her truck, hollering, "Don't forget your camera. I have suntan lotion and dinner."

Without talking, we turned and ran to the bedroom. I grabbed my camera and a ball cap. Mateo came out with his camera and a silver-studded, wide-rimmed, black felt cowboy hat with a chin strap. I'd never seen him wear this one. Mateo said, "I came prepared for wind and sun."

We raced to the truck and jumped in. "Nice boat. Is it your dad's?" I couldn't lie as the truck, trailer, and the boat put me over-the-top jealous.

"Nope, all mine. It's a 2014 Jimmy White Airboat. I saved for two years to get it. I was going to take Gram on our Sunday ride, but when I got there, she told me about you guys and that she owed you. We are getting a late start, but we'll have a few hours. It doesn't get dark until around seven-thirty.

Mateo quickly corrected Emmie, "Violet doesn't owe us, and we will gladly contribute for your time and gas."

"Gram said you guys helped her board up the house. She already paid for the gas and bought us chicken dinner. I love it out in the glades, so there's no need to *contribute*," Emmie emphasized her last word and then giggled. "I don't have to ask which of you is the writer because I can see the cowboy, but you guys could tell me about yourselves."

She listened and seemed truly interested. It only took twenty minutes before we pulled into a small but busy parking area with a boat launch that dropped you into what appeared to be a canal. She pulled the truck around and backed in like no problem at all.

Mateo helped her with the boat while I took pictures of them and the red and white airboat. The airboat had a couch-style double seat with two tall seats directly behind. There were two vertical fins behind the caged propeller blades.

Emmie parked the truck and trailer. Once we boarded, she reached into a box filled with earmuffs and handed us each a pair before starting the motor.

I'm sure the muffs were meant to block noise, but I wanted to get the full effect. I didn't put them on.

She had no mercy for us and took off like a streak of lightning. We headed north, which surprised me. I loved the ocean and would've headed south.

The sound of the blades started loud and escalated into a roaring hum. I put the ear protection in place and noticed that Emmie tried to hide a grin. The force of the wind made Mateo hold his hat. We hadn't gone very far when she slowed and made a turn, off the wide canal, into what appeared a less-traveled route. She slowed way down when we saw herons and egrets. I snapped some pictures.

We took an overgrown path that was a jungle of succulents, cacti, hanging moss, and tall grass. The everglades weren't like I thought. I didn't realize there would be so much land area amid all the water and reeds. When we spotted small deer, Emmie cut the engine and let us float. I also got a real close-up of a ginormous alligator. "This gator makes me think of a dog begging for food at the dinner table."

"He is begging for food." Emmie opened a plastic bin beside her seat and tossed the gator a chicken leg. The second the meat hit its tongue the mouth instantly slammed shut. "The airboat tour guides often feed them."

She started the motor again, and we rode around for about an hour. We came to a clearing where Emmie didn't spare the speed and did some side turns that made us shout out and hang on. At one point, Mateo turned and hollered something to her, pointing at some brush that we headed toward.

Emmie nodded and gave him a big smile. With her gestures, she told us to hang on. We grabbed for the armrests and back of the seat because she wasn't changing course. She increased speed, and we hit that brush, caught some air, then landed with a thud and a splash. We all hooted. I think they laughed because they liked the thrill. I laughed because I was glad that we lived through it.

Slowing again, Emmie drove the boat right up on land. She cut the engine and pulled out paper plates, chicken, coleslaw, and french fries.

Breathing in the heavy air that smelled of soil and plant life, made me feel relaxed in a weird kind of way. Maybe this was what God intended life to be like, so wild and free.

Mateo got off the boat, carrying his plateful to a nearby tree. "What kind of weird tree is this?"

Emmie answered, "It's called a Mangrove tree, and you're sitting on part of the root system. The roots of these trees are above ground more than under."

I set my plate on the seat and had my camera strapped around my neck so that I could grab it in a hurry. "I read that December through April is a dry season and the best time to visit the Everglades. The weather report shows some storms out to sea but not headed this way, so why is your grandma boarding up her house?"

"I've learned never to doubt that lady. She's seldom wrong and always prepared."

Mateo called out, "I found a snake. It's beautiful, but I think it is poisonous. Looks like a Coral Snake."

We got off the boat and rushed to see. The snake moved slowly through the underbrush, not at all in a hurry.

Emmie said, "The color is similar to a coral snake, which is red-on-yellow stripes, but this guy is red-on-black, which makes it a scarlet kingsnake. It is not venomous." She picked it up. "Do you guys like to fish?"

We each took a step away before answering that we would like to do some fishing.

Emmie played with the snake and said, "Sometimes Gram and I bring fishing poles out here. We always bring lunch and usually stop right here in this same spot because the water is a little deeper, which means good fishing." She glanced around. "I don't like to be here in the evening. That's when the predators come out." She put the snake in some tall grass. We watched it slither away.

Emmie threw her half-eaten chicken leg into the brush, and in the silence, we could hear strange bird calls and other unfamiliar noises. "I'm taking my boat to the marina instead of loading it on the trailer. I have friends there who will take us back to pick up my truck. It will be a lot of monkeying around, but I think we will be using the boat a lot." Then she pointed at Mateo and asked, "What have you seen that you liked the most, here in the Everglades?"

"The fearless way you handled that boat when you jumped that brush. I was glad to be hanging on."

"I would have done some fast stops to soak you both but was afraid for the cameras."

"Boy, am I glad you didn't," I said. "What kind of fish do you catch?"

"There are all kinds, but I usually hook sea trout, bluegill, and largemouth bass. What do you think about fishing next weekend?"

"Why not tomorrow?"

"I have to work all week. But we could make a day of it Saturday. Gram would love to come, too. Right now, we better head home. It will be dark before long."

It would be a very long week after such a fun and helpful afternoon. Although, it might take me that long to write about everything I'd seen.

CHAPTER SEVEN

The Truck

Silence filled the house. A glance at Mateo's empty bed made me wonder where he went. I checked around for my phone and found it on the floor beside the bed. I must have fallen asleep after talking to Mom and Dad.

My phone battery only had a half charge, and Haylee had texted again. This time, I texted her about our exciting trip to the Everglades yesterday and that we might walk there today.

After getting dressed, I searched the house for Mateo with no luck. I made some peanut butter toast and went outside. The birds in Florida were so beautiful in color and song. Little lizards scurried away with every step I took. I couldn't wait to get into the Everglades again.

Around the side of the house, I found Mateo seated on the cement driveway with the boat motor torn apart. "What are you doing?"

"Steve said that we could use this motor if we fixed it. Didn't you have a great time yesterday? I did, and I want to go fishing today."

"You make me laugh. Of course, I want to go. You think you can fix it?" A new excitement shot me into overdrive. But how would we get the boat and motor to the Everglades? I turned toward the truck parked just off the driveway with thick grass growing around it.

"The keys are in it." Mateo stood up, pointing at the truck. "It started, but we have to roll the rear tire into town to get air."

"Steve didn't say that we could take the truck." Guilt ravaged me, just thinking about taking the vehicle without permission.

"He said if we fixed the boat's motor, we could use it. How else would we use it if we didn't take the truck?" Mateo got a little louder with each word, and his eyebrows made wrinkles above his nose.

"Well, that's true." My friend had a point, and we wouldn't be gone very long. "So, when are you going to put the motor back together?" We were doing Steve a favor by fixing the boat motor and the truck tire. I would mow the lawn to help pay for the use of his stuff.

"I already took the tire off, but we need to get a carburetor kit. So, don't get all excited because I'm not a hundred percent sure that will fix the motor."

"Oh." My enthusiasm bombed out. "Before we go to town, we should thank Emmie's grandmother."

"Violet's house is in the opposite direction, and it's almost eight o'clock. Let's go see her tomorrow morning?"

"Okay." I stuffed the last bite of toast in my mouth, walked around the truck, and rolled the tire toward the sidewalk.

Mateo ran into the house, back out in seconds, grabbed the carburetor, and we headed to town.

We would have more to tell Violet tomorrow anyway. "Where did you find the tools?" I asked.

"He had a small toolbox in the boat and, planned to, or had been working on the motor. I also found a couple of fishing poles under the boat seat."

I smiled about the poles, hoping we would get to use them. My body ached from being bent-over as

I rolled the tire. "How do you know you need a kit to fix the carburetor?"

"I checked to see if the plugs sparked, and they did, so that tells me the carburetor might not be getting the gas to the motor. My grandpa is good at small engine repair and lets me help."

We were almost to the gas station, and I noticed a boat dealer just ahead. I nudged Mateo and pointed. "Would that boat place have a kit?"

"Looks like today is our lucky day."

We filled the tire with air, and I bought some live bait: a dozen crawlers and a bag full of live shrimp. Mateo bought the kit from the boat dealer. I was so excited I forgot about my aches and pains as I rolled the tire back to Steve's house.

I replaced the tire, moved the truck and trailer, and mowed the small yard while Mateo put the boat motor together. He picked up the motor and put it in the barrel of water, where we had originally found it.

"You have to start the motor in water, or you'll burn up the water pump. Here we go." Mateo pulled the starter rope. It sputtered. He pulled again, and it started. So he shut it off, and together, we put it on the rear of the boat.

We raced inside the house to grab necessities, like a big lunch with lots of snack food and drinks because we'd probably be out most of the day.

Emmie had warned about staying into the evening, so no sense packing more than that. I grabbed towels, sunscreen, and my hat. The last thing was to write a note just in case Steve came while we were gone.

The drive to the boat launch seemed short, and the truck's motor purred like a kitten. Mateo backed the boat in, and we easily got it off the trailer.

"Oh man, I forgot to put the oars in the boat. They are leaning against the fence at Steve's." Mateo looked worried and a bit embarrassed.

"So what's the big problem? We have the motor. Why would we need to have the oars?"

"For one, you need the oars to push off the shore. And what if we have to ward off an alligator?" He still wore a worried look, even though I thought he was joking about the alligator.

"We can do this. You get in and take care of the motor. I'll park the truck, and then push us off."

After parking, I got a little wet pushing us offshore. The water got deep right away, making it hard to get into the boat, but the motor started without any problem. We headed north just like Emmie had.

Mateo was right. This was our lucky day.

My shin hurt from getting in the boat, so I rubbed it. "Where are we going to fish?"

"I liked the place Emmie took us. She said that it would be good fishing there, and we could move if we aren't catching anything."

"Good idea. She knows the best places." I pointed up. "It's getting cloudy. That's good. We won't get a glare off the water." We could hear birds but didn't see many.

Mateo drove slow just in case we would get the opportunity to get a good picture, but we didn't see much worthy of a photograph. Then it hit me.

"Mateo. Maybe Violet was right."

"What do you mean?"

"I mean, maybe she was right about a storm. Gators head to deeper water when a storm is coming and most animals take cover. We haven't seen any critters." I looked up at the sky. "It's cloudy and feels like rain."

"Aw, you worry too much. We're almost to the fishing hole, and it's not raining now."

I pushed back on the uneasy flutter in my stomach and focused on this wild world around me. We had invaded the natural uncivilized world, and it was exciting. I glanced at Mateo, who seemed tuned-in with nature, too.

"I think the spot we want is just around this curve." The adventurer in me needed to explore.

CHAPTER EIGHT

Good Fishin'

Mateo and I moved through trails of water separated by grassy marsh to more like a river with woods on either side. The canopy of trees over the water made me think of a tunnel. The wildlife, no longer hidden from view, overran this patch of forest. White birds flew in groups just ahead, and gators lay on the water's edge, eyeing us as we puttered around the bend.

"There's that big mangrove you sat on yesterday." I noticed several more mangrove and palmetto trees all around the big one. Mateo gunned the motor just before he shut it down. That way, the boat slid up on land. I jumped out and hauled it farther onto solid earth.

I pulled out the tackle box and fishing poles and watched Mateo head for the woods. "Where are you going?"

"We both need a walking stick." Mateo must have changed his mind because he rushed back, grabbed the can of bug spray, and used it on his clothes, head and face, and arms. "You better put some on right away. They are thick today."

"Why do we need walking sticks?" I took the spray and used it.

"We might need to fight a gator. Look across the water." Mateo pointed at a log on the other side, maybe fifteen or twenty feet away.

First, I saw a Blue Heron that appeared frozen in time. It stood poised perfectly still, with its neck stretched out, ready to strike any unsuspecting fish. Then I noticed a log with three giant turtles, and on the bank, six huge gators. I gasped for air.

"Don't get a flimsy stick that will break. Check for hardwood." I didn't wait for Mateo to return. Both of the fishing poles had cork bobbers and a weird rig for the hook. I chose the pole with the smaller cork bobber, slipped on a shrimp, and cast it out. Before it even had time to settle to the bottom, I had a major bite. I jerked, and the fight was on.

My arm grew weak before I got that fighter to the bank. I stepped into the water, grabbed the fish by the gill, turned, and held up that foot-long redfish to show Mateo. "Hey, look!"

His eyes got big, and he screamed, "Look behind you."

Two gators had left the opposite bank. They didn't appear to be coming across…at least not yet. "Hurry up with our swords." I jumped out of the water, pulled the stringer out of the tackle box, and slid the metal ring over a broken-off tree limb. "First one of the day!"

I checked my phone for the time, noticed I didn't have any bars, and there wasn't much charge left. "It's already one-thirty." Mateo handed me the perfect club, around four or five feet long like his and big enough to do some damage if necessary.

Mateo took the big bobber off his pole. He cast out, reeling slow and consistent to keep the worm moving. He fished for bass. I fished for whatever bit. The alligators moved in every time we caught a fish but never got close enough for us to use the clubs. *I think I'd give them the fish and skip battling a gator with nothing more than a club.*

My stomach knotted up. The phone screen showed four o'clock. "We forgot to eat lunch, and it's almost dinner time." I placed the cooler on the middle seat of the boat, which seemed like the perfect place to sit. We both ate a grocery store sub. Even though the bread was soggy, it tasted good.

"We've got about a dozen fish to clean. I think that's enough for a couple of meals, so how about throwing back any more that we catch?" Mateo threw the last bite of his sandwich to the gators. They thrashed about fighting for that nibble.

"Sounds like an environmental thing to do."

Something coughed from the weeds behind the trees. Then a raspy noise came from the same place. Mateo's eyebrows furrowed with a questioning survey of the area.

"That might be an iguana." I got out of the boat. "They cough and sneeze to get rid of the salt build-up from eating the leaves of the mangrove. Let's go see." I grabbed my stick.

Mateo beat me over there. When he poked his stick into the weeds, a mess of iguana fled in every direction. Some were huge, like four feet long. We both jumped and quickly made our way to the boat. I wished I had taken my camera, so once in the boat, I hung it around my neck.

The fish never stopped biting, and I lost count of how many I threw back.

Mateo hollered, "I've got a big fish on." The bent pole told the same story. He fought, pulled with his whole body, then leaned forward, and reeled fast and hard. The fish blasted right out of the water. "Shark!"

Mateo fought hard, but when that big fish slammed into the water, the line snapped, and that fish was gone.

"I got a great picture of the shark in mid-air. He's a young one."

"Does the picture show me, too?"

"Yes, and the gators across the way. Best picture ever." I handed the camera to Mateo so he could see.

"Sorry that you lost the shark."

"I'm not. How would you get the hook out of a shark's mouth? This will be a great story to tell everyone with a picture to prove it." He returned the camera.

"It's almost seven. We'd better hurry. Time sure does fly here. Do you want to come again tomorrow?"

"Yeah, sure do. We will get an earlier start and visit Violet first."

I put the food and empty soda cans in the cooler, dropped the stringer full of fish in the bottom of the boat, and emptied the remainder of bait in the water. "I'm going to keep my walking stick."

Mateo put his stick in the boat, too, and got in. He moved to the rear of the boat and pulled the rope to start the motor. It sputtered, so he yanked the cord again. It didn't start.

"Are you kidding me?" I couldn't hide the terror in my voice.

He worked at starting the motor for a long time before getting out of the boat. "No sense to keep trying. It's flooded. I can't believe I left the oars."

"Would it matter? We couldn't have rowed back this late in the day anyway. Too far. We don't have much time before dark. We had better prepare for the night. There's no time to waste." My voice sounded frantic, which matched how I felt.

"Take a chill. We got this. First thing, we will need a fire for warmth and protection, so clear an area not too far away and make a pit with stones around it." Mateo headed into the wooded area. "I'll get some wood."

I moved away from the water and trees, then pulled weeds and brush out of the ground. I had seen some rocks near the water and gathered a few of them to surround the pit. Working helped keep the fear away.

Mateo returned with an armload of wood and said, "Let's get the boat close to the pit. That's where we will sleep."

"In the boat?"

"We might have to deal with snakes, insects, and who knows what else. The boat seems like the safest place. I'll take the motor off, and we'll pull the boat over here." Mateo walked over and waded into the water to take off the motor. I helped carry it to the big mangrove tree.

We removed everything out of the boat, except the fish, and dragged it toward the firepit. Mateo didn't look at all frightened. "Did you make the pit far enough back?" he grumbled.

"When I made the pit, I didn't think about dragging a boat. What are we going to use to light the fire?"

"A lighter," Mateo said, reaching into his pants' pocket. "Now we know why your dad wanted someone smart to go with you."

CHAPTER NINE

Night

Dusk settled in, and so did the mosquitoes. We still had to take the fish down to the water's edge to clean them. It would be a bad idea to have the smell of fish guts in our sleeping area. Mateo had a great fire started, and I just wanted to take off these wet socks.

A few paces before we got to the water's edge, we heard a big splash. My skin prickled with goosebumps, and I came to a dead stop. "What was that?"

"It doesn't matter. We have to clean these fish. We know something heard us coming and left." He slapped a mosquito on his other hand.

Frogs or maybe some kind of insects sang loud and clear, making me think of a Disney musical. We rushed to clean the fish while fighting the buzzing pests. Mateo left the heads on the fish, made a slit down the belly, then handed each one to me. I scraped out the guts and rinsed them in the river.

I heard a commotion on the opposite side of the water. "Two more to go. Should we stand by the fire? We have enough." I waved away the bugs and wondered what was coming.

"No, we can finish. You don't know how long we'll be here. We might need the fish you want to leave."

We finished the last two and headed to relief. I hurried in front of Mateo when a growl erupted into a fight. The night hid what happened behind us, but fire lit the area directly around the pit. We ran to that safe place, a haven even from the mosquitoes.

"We have to cook all these fish, and what we don't eat, let's put in the cooler. It's important to keep this area clean of food," Mateo handed me a long stick. "Push the stick through the mouth and out the bottom by the tail." He demonstrated then added, "We'll roast three to a stick."

"First, I have to get these socks off. I've had wet feet ever since I caught that first fish." I draped the wet socks over the rim of the boat and sat on a big piece of wood by the fire, roasting the first three fish. The dirt still felt warm, but the air was cooling. From my research, I knew it would probably get down to the low sixties tonight.

"Now that we have the most important stuff handled, you better call your dad and tell him where Violet lives. He can call the cops. Even though we don't know her last name, they will know Violet by the clues we give your dad. She will call Emmie, and we will be found."

I slowly lowered my head, not wanting to say the horrible truth out loud.

"What's wrong?"

After pulling the phone from my pocket, I tossed it to him. He studied it, whistled, and said, "Yeeha, we're in it now." He threw it back. "Not only no signal, but you don't have much battery life either. Maybe you should turn it off to conserve what little power you still have."

"At least, it didn't rain." What a stupid thing to say, but I had no excuses—nothing positive to share. Our lives were in danger, and what did I do but say a few more stupid things. "What if we can't get the motor started? Nobody knows we're out here."

He stared at the fire while turning his skewer of fish. All we could hear was the music of the night critters. We sat like that for a long time. Finally,

Mateo walked to the cooler, placed some fronds on top of the ice, and then pulled off each fish, laying it on the fern leaves. He cast a glance my way. "Yours should be done, too."

After putting mine in the cooler, we refilled our sticks with more fish, and then I put my shoes on.

Mateo finally responded, "Look, you're not the only one that is scared, so let's act like we're camping out for the night and try to make it fun. It is nice by the fire. Someone will come around sooner or later."

I broke off a piece of fish, blew on it, and took a nibble. "Man, this is good!"

Mateo smiled and ate, too. "There are four pops left and we can drink the water from the ice. Do you think we should have one tonight?"

"No, I think we should be really careful with our drinks. The river water has salt in it. It's called brackish, and we can't drink it. We will probably get picked up tomorrow by someone, but we should ration what we have until we know for sure. Well, except for the Twinkies, we have plenty." We both laughed.

Mateo opened the cooler, took out a piece of ice, and popped it in his mouth. "You want one too?" He threw more wood on the fire until it blazed up into the night.

I ate a piece of ice, too. On my return to the fire, I grabbed the towels, handed one to Mateo, and draped mine around my shoulders. "It's getting chilly. Good thing we brought these. So, are we going to take turns sleeping, or do you think we're safe?"

"I don't know. The fire should keep most everything away, but I'm not sure about snakes. Remember the super snakes Violet mentioned? There's not much that I'm afraid of, but I hate snakes. The fire might die down if we both slept, so let's take turns."

We moved into the boat as an extra measure of safety after hearing some crashing nearby. Mateo said it sounded like deer. We never said who would take the first watch, but Mateo fell asleep. I put more wood on the fire and had my walking stick with me all the time.

I studied the edge of darkness and thought about how mad my dad was right about now. I hadn't called tonight, but he would be able to tell my phone was shut off. I wonder what he would do when I didn't call in the morning, either.

Thoughts of Haylee, the horses, all my rodeo friends, school, and a million other things swirled through my brain. I prayed for my mom. I believed that she might be sicker than they had told me. Part of me felt guilty for coming here without her. I scanned the area and pictured my mom here. What a laugh. She would never be out here, day or night.

Maybe Emmie would drive past Steve's house and notice the boat was gone. Maybe Steve would come home and find the note, but how could he find us. The Everglades covered a vast area.

My eyes grew heavy. I fought sleep for a long time but finally woke Mateo to take over.

Day 2

Mateo stood by the water laughing. I followed the direction of his gaze and saw a beautiful Pink Spoonbill with the weirdest beak. I sat up and glanced around.

No sun again today, but very warm and humid. The temperature hadn't dropped during the night like I thought it would, and now heavy dark clouds filled the sky. Getting out of the boat took effort. I would never, again, take my bed for granted.

The fire raged. Mateo must have just filled the pit with wood. *Why would he burn up so much wood this early in the day?* The cooler lay open and upside down, with food remnants and Twinkie wrappers scattered everywhere.

I hurried to the river. "What happened to the cooler?"

Mateo was tying a slip knot, making a lasso out of the fishing line. He pointed at the little footprints everywhere. "I fell asleep last night. "Looks like raccoon tracks. The coons probably made the growling and fighting sounds we heard last night. Anyway, we have to eat, so I'm going to catch a few iguanas. Then we'll have to do some more fishing and get ready for the storm."

"How long do you think before the storm hits?"

"I'm hoping after dinner," Mateo said.

"It was stupid, but I threw out the leftover bait when we packed up yesterday, so I'll search for bait now." I walked over to the cooler and put the sodas back inside it. "Looks like they tried to open the cans. Lucky for us, they aren't that smart. They must have dragged one of the cans away. There's only three here." My parched throat begged to open a can.

"I drank one. Had to."

"Okay, I'll drink one now, too. It's probably smart."

"Yesterday, after cutting some thick vines, I noticed clear liquid oozing out, so I tried it. The liquid did not taste bitter, so I drank enough that we would be able to tell in a few hours if it was toxic." He took the pole, grabbed his walking stick, and headed into the brush. "Want to help me catch the iguanas? By the time we catch and clean a few, the coals should be ready."

After putting my shoes on and grabbing my camera and stick, I followed.

A big iguana sat up bobbing its head, maybe to make itself appear larger. Watching Mateo in action reminded me of how good he was at being a cowboy. He could rope and ride as good as any grown man. I took pictures as he slipped that looped fishing line over the iguana's head and pulled it tight. Quick and easy, he had that critter dangling.

Mateo held the wiggling creature with one hand and in the other, the fishing pole that now doubled as an iguana catcher. "You've got two choices. You can take this critter down to the river, kill, and clean it, or you can take the pole and catch the next one."

Neither alternative sounded good, so I took the best choice of the two and grabbed the pole. "I'll catch the next one."

Mateo headed to the river holding the iguana by the tail. I hung my camera on a tree limb.

His laughter made me mad. I guessed he didn't think I could catch one. A young iguana raced around a palmetto tree. I tried to catch up, but when I rounded the tree, a five-foot iguana met me with a determined look in its eyes.

The next thing I knew, the line had looped its head, and I pulled. I hadn't thought that maybe its size could be a problem. This guy did not want to be captured and fought like a banshee. "Mateo," I screamed. "Get over here and help me."

The monster iguana rolled and made weird noises. The force of his roll jerked me right off my feet, but I held on, got up, and pulled that demon out of the woods.

Mateo came on a run, tossed the dead iguana near the firepit, and joined me. I didn't know what to do with this wild animal.

"Get a little closer to him, and he'll wear himself out. When he stops flailing, pull the loop tight, and drag him to the river."

"Forget that. Hit it with your stick." My jaw dropped open. "You might get a thrill out of danger and probable body damage, but I do not."

"It's huge. Why did you pick a giant?"

****

We roasted the iguanas by splaying them out on the glowing coals. I wasn't sure about eating meat covered with ash, but we had to. Mateo turned the big one with his knife, cooking the other side.

I snapped pictures of the cooking food and the darkening sky. Heavy black clouds headed our way. "Before we find bait for fishing, we should flip the boat over for cover from the rain. We are in for a big storm."

Mateo pointed and made gestures with his hands. "How about we move the boat behind the big mangrove and block it between two of the smaller mangroves?"

"But then no one would see us if, by chance, someone went by."

"I don't think anyone is going to be on a pleasure cruise today. My first thought was to leave the boat by the fire, but with our luck, swirling winds would shower us with hot coals." He took the small iguana off the fire and cut it in half.

Showing teeth, I took a bite of the hind leg. "Not too bad. A little chewy and could use salt, but it will fill our bellies and give us protein."

The wind came up and sent sparks flying. It seemed like nature exhibited Mateo's point about the coals. He pulled the giant iguana out, laid it on the log we usually sat on, grabbed the emptied cooler, and headed to the river. "Let's fill this up and douse those coals. It's possible that if we don't, this whole area could go up in flames. I think we'd better hurry."

Still chewing the last of my half of cooked iguana, I rushed to help him lug the heavy, water-filled cooler back to the pit. The coals spat, popped, and smoked before dying down. Stirring the coals with my walking stick proved that we had to make another trip.

Across the river, alligators ease into the water. No birds were around, and it had gotten quiet. We doused the coals again, and it started to sprinkle. I picked up the rear end of the boat, with Mateo at the front. We half carried, half dragged it behind the biggest mangrove and, then wedged it between two other mangrove trees.

"The storm is coming from the south, so let's lift the north side so we can see, and the boat will be a shield from behind," I said.

"Hey, we almost forgot the towels. The tool chest and tackle box should be okay where they are." Mateo pulled the damp towels from a tree on the other side of the pit. He returned and stuffed them between the bottom of the boat and the upside-down seats. I put my camera there too, but not touching the towels.

Mateo ran to get the cooked iguana while I shoved the cooler under the boat and pushed a small log into our makeshift home so we wouldn't have to sit on the sure-to-get-wet ground.

We were thinking and acting like a well-practiced team.

Lightning cracked, and thunder boomed in the distance. The black clouds dropping rain inched closer, but we stood, watching this nightmarish scene advance. Then, at the last moment, we ducked under the boat for protection.

CHAPTER ELEVEN

Emmie Searches

"Emmie, come and eat." Gramma Violet carried a bottle of wine into the dining room. The table held more food than we would eat in a week. "I thought maybe those boys might drop in today, and I would ask them to dinner. I never dreamed you'd come on a Monday, but it worked out wonderfully."

"After work, my car headed in this direction. I had nothing to do with it." I took a seat across from Gram. "The weatherman sounded like we might get a crippling storm tomorrow. The weather report added to the fact that you had the windows boarded-up, prompted a day off. I needed a day away from Miami anyway."

"I don't think those boys have any idea of how bad a Florida storm can be. I hope they will be all right."

"I stopped by Steve's before I came here. Maybe they heard the weather report and returned to Michigan because there wasn't a soul around there." I scooped out some potatoes and handed the bowl to Gram.

"We're all set for the storm with the windows boarded and the pantry stocked."

"After tomorrow's storm, let's take a boat ride for fun and see if our fishing hole is still there. I'll check with the boys in the morning to see if they want to go."

****

Late morning, I stretched and rolled over. It felt so good to sleep in, but I could smell coffee.

"Emmie, you'd better hurry if you're going to check on those boys. The weather reports that the winds and rain should hit within the hour."

I dressed, brushed my hair, and started down the stairs before answering, "Is it okay with you if I bring those guys back here with me? It does sound like we're in for some severe weather."

"You don't even have to ask. There's enough food in the refrigerator to feed an army."

Instead of walking, I drove the short distance just in case the rain came earlier than predicted. I pulled to the curb in front of Steve's house. No lights on in the place, but maybe they were still sleeping. I got out and knocked on the door, then found a piece of paper and a pen in my purse and wrote an invitation to hurry over.

The rain let loose as I pulled into Gram's driveway. Running into the house didn't prevent the rain from soaking my hair and clothes.

Gram stared at the television, taking in every word while watching the radar. "Stay where you are." Gram grabbed a towel from the linen closet and brought it to me before heading toward the dining room. "I think we'd better get out an oil lamp. Hope I don't lose my trees."

I followed her in case she needed a hand. The lantern sat on top of the china hutch, so I pulled out the step stool, climbed onto it, and carefully eased the light down. "There. I'll put it on the table."

I would have loved to look out the window, but the boys and Gram took care of that. The sound of the wind and loud claps of thunder reverberated throughout the house.

Gram put a book of matches near the glass lamp. "We haven't even gotten the worst of the wind yet. Once the first portion of the storm has passed, we will have most of the day to clean up before we get hit again late this afternoon."

"If we're getting another storm in the afternoon, then why would we pick up after the first one?" I had to raise my voice because she had the TV so loud.

"I guess we could leave it all to fly around in the second half of the storm and possibly ruin the siding or roof." Gram gave me one of her sly smiles like I should have known better than to have said something so ridiculous.

The storm's fury lasted for at least an hour before letting up. Curiosity had the better of me, so I opened the front door to see how much work the wind had left us. I shut it and took my seat near Gram.

"Well, how bad is it?"

"Not at all." I lied.

Gram headed to the back door. "Oh, my goodness, grab two pairs of gloves. We've got work to do."

"Look at the Wilsons' house." I pointed at the tree that had crashed on top of the neighbor's house. "Let's go see if they're all right. I hope Mateo and Mitchell are okay. I'll check on them later."

Gram stood in front of me and knocked on Mrs. Wilson's door. A few minutes passed before a frail older lady opened it. "Look at you two, come in, come in. Fred is in the living room, calling for help."

A tree branch had come through the roof and into their living room. Fred Wilson spoke into the phone receiver, giving his address.

It had been a long time since I'd seen someone use a landline phone and doubly shocked that it worked after the storm. I turned to Mrs. Wilson. "We are going to do some picking up around Gram's house. How about you and Mr. Wilson come over anyway?"

Gram picked up on my invitation and added, "Yes, Freida. I won't take no for an answer. Pack a bag and plan on staying until they get this mess cleaned up."

"Oh, thank you. We might just do that."

They had help coming, so we went back to assessing Gram's damages. Except for a lot of branches, there was no devastation like next door.

After creating piles of sticks and branches at the side of the house, I said, "I'm going to check on Mateo and Mitchell." It didn't look like we would get rain right away, so I walked. Several of the homes showed damage, and everyone had branches down.

Steve's house didn't appear damaged but still dark, and my saturated note lay plastered on the ground behind the bushes. I knocked anyway. No answer. *They must have returned to Michigan or maybe felt safer in Miami.* Then I noticed that

Steve's boat was no longer parked at the side of the driveway. *What if...* I hurried back to Gram's house.

"Let's take an airboat ride before the next storm moves in," I suggested.

"I'm not sure we're going to get another storm, but you could go look. I'll wait here for the Wilsons'."

Once at the marina, I worried that I might have a problem getting to my boat or trouble returning. Some men were working by the docks, so just in case there was trouble, I told them my name and that I would be taking my boat out for an hour or so. One of the men wrote the information down. Then I got in my boat and took off.

The nice thing about an airboat was that you could fly over debris, and I did. I drove right to my fishing area and almost cried. I turned the boat around then sat staring at my big mangrove tree. A split down the middle had left half of the tree in a heap on the ground. Several other trees had also been uprooted.

I had thought the boys might have come out here with Steve's boat, but it wasn't here either. Tears streaked down my cheeks. I wiped them away and headed back, not knowing if I could ever return to that horrible mess. *What would I tell Gram?*

CHAPTER TWELVE

Storm

Sheets of rain pounded the aluminum boat. Strange sounds whined and roared making me wonder if the noise came from rain or the wind. Trees danced and bent low, which made me worry about those around us.

Not only mosquitoes but palmetto bugs and centipedes wanted to share our safe area. "Where's the bug spray?" I asked.

"It's in the toolbox by the big mangrove tree. I don't want to go out there."

"Me either, but I will." I pointed at the cooler. "We should be catching rainwater to drink." I ducked, slid out from underneath the boat then ran, grabbing the toolbox and tackle box.

I climbed under the boat and found that Mateo had emptied the cooler, leaving the lid open and, leaned it against the tree just outside the boat. Rainwater already covered the bottom. I used a towel to dry my hair while shaking the rain off my body. We sprayed ourselves with the bug repellent choking on the fumes.

"Hey, look." Mateo pointed at the ground. Tons of worms wiggled out and squirmed under leaves.

"They always do that in a rainstorm. People used to think worms came out of the ground when it rained because they would drown, but the truth is, rain makes a vibration similar to that of a predator, like a mole digging."

"Not so many bugs now. Thanks for braving the weather to get the spray. Man, that wind is scary." Right after Mateo said those words, a huge crack of thunder sounded somewhere behind us.

We could only see in front of us toward the fire pit, which quickly became a pond. A tree just beyond the fire pit crashed to the ground uprooted by the wind. I wondered if my eyes widened as much as my friend's.

Strengthening my voice so Mateo could hear, I asked, "Are you sorry you came with me?"

"Yeah, nothing could be scarier than being stranded in the everglades in a tropical storm." He kicked at a giant spider. "But this storm will probably be something I talk about for the rest of my life, so I should say thank you."

The smile not only covered my face but my heart, too. "Do you think you'll ever eat iguana again?"

"Hate to tell you, but we are eating the monster iguana for lunch. Hopefully, the storm lets up, so we can do some fishing."

The hair on my arms stood on end, and at the same time, my scalp felt tingly. Thunder boomed so loud that I threw my hands over my ears. I knew the lightning must have hit a nearby tree, but I was afraid to get out from under the boat. Thank God we weren't touching the aluminum.

Only seconds passed when an explosion of splintering wood rang out. Leaves crashed into view, the ground shook, and a tree landed right in front of the boat. So close that we would have to crawl through the branches to get out.

My throat swelled, and tears streaked down my face. A horrible choking sound came from deep inside me. My body wouldn't stop shaking.

Mateo didn't cry. He put his arm around my shoulder. "We're all right. We're all right. Calm down. It's okay."

The storm raged while I fought to get myself under control. It seemed that all the pent-up fear and uncertainty escaped to embarrass me in front of my best friend. As the wind and rain calmed, so did I. The birds, on the other hand, made a loud outcry of what might have been a show of happiness. They outdid themselves with beautiful songs.

After wiping my face and inhaling deeply, I found my voice. "Want to see what the storm left us?" I pulled my camera out from its hiding place.

I lost sight of Mateo in a sea of green leaves as he crawled through part of the downed tree. After making my way behind him, I stood and took stock of the damage. That big beautiful mangrove tree near the river had a blackened split down the top center. A big section of the tree now lay in front of the boat.

"We were lucky the tree didn't crush us," Mateo pointed to where the firepit had been. We now had a small lake filled with sticks and leaves instead of our pit.

"How are we going to have a fire tonight?" Suddenly another type of fear tore through me. *Nighttime*, which meant animals would stalk the area to find food. "We need fire to cook and keep away predators."

"We have to make a new firepit, but we'll worry about that later. The first thing we need to do is to find and uncover the cooler. I need a drink." He pulled on a big branch, but it was all connected to the main limb and too big to cut up with a pocket knife.

"How about we climb back through to the boat? The cooler should be just outside at the front end of the boat." This time Mateo followed me.

We couldn't stand up. Instead, I tilted the ice chest forward. We took turns cupping our hands to contain the water and drink. We ate the meat while we were near the cooler.

"The next thing we need to do is search for bugs or larva to use for fishing. I hope the poles are okay. The last time I saw them, they were propped against the lightning tree. We better bring the tackle box out of here too. I need a new hook," Mateo said. "Remember that shark shooting out of the water? That was so cool, but he took my hook with him."

The way in and out of the boat area had become more like an overgrown path now. The poles were right where we'd left them.

"I saw some palmetto bug larva yesterday over there." I pointed, but nothing looked the same. We stepped over tree branches and searched under rocks for grasshoppers or whatever might attract a fish. I found the palmetto tree and the yellow larva of the bugs.

Fishing wasn't as easy as yesterday because the fish were full of all the worms and bugs that had washed into the water after the storm. The gators were gone, and herons fished nearby. Mateo caught four fish, while I only caught two. But that amount would fill our bellies.

"Don't you wonder what everyone thinks because they haven't heard from us?" I asked.

"Both of our families will be camped out at Steve's house by the time we get out of here. They will be so happy to see us it won't matter that we stole Steve's boat and truck."

"What? We didn't steal anything. You said, that he said, we could take it."

"Well, he did. Kind of...say that."

"My dad will kill me." I picked up some firewood and followed Mateo.

"No, I already told you. Our families will be so relieved to see us they won't even be mad. They will be angry with Steve, who will be so busy defending himself he won't have time to be mad at us either."

We talked while we made a new fire pit closer to the river on high ground.

"Hope you're right, but I don't think it will work out like that." I didn't say anything for a few minutes, thinking about seeing my family and feeling safe again. Then a thought came to mind. "I don't worry about getting out of here. I know we will because we've done a good job of staying alive so far."

Mateo handed me his pocket knife and some wet but dead pieces of wood. "Shave off small chunks of this while I look for a bird nest or fuzz from the palmetto trees. Either of those will help start the fire. Then we'll slowly add the small pieces you're cutting. Everything is so wet. I hope we can start this fire."

I chopped the small pieces right into the new pit. I looked in Mateo's direction at the same time I heard him scream.

CHAPTER THIRTEEN

The Python

Mateo's shrill scream shocked me. I grabbed my camera and bolted into action to see what could scare a guy like him. Brave and fearless were two words that came to mind when one would think of Mateo. My mind moved faster than my feet, and halfway there, I knew it was a snake. That was the only thing I'd seen that frightened him.

What I saw almost made me scream. A Burmese Python wrapped around a baby pig, preparing to eat. You would think the pig would have been squealing, but the snake had squeezed it so tight that its eyes bulged from their sockets. I'm pretty sure that little pig couldn't make any noise.

Dark brown splotches covered the snake's thick body. I would guess if you stretched the snake out, it would be at least fifteen feet in length. We stood too close but luckily it had already found dinner.

"Kill it." Mateo choked out.

The knife, still in my hand, wouldn't even get close to the python because I could not make myself advance on something so big and powerful. I shook my head and grunted no.

Mesmerized, we watched the slow progress of the snake eating the wild hog. First, it moved the pig around so that the snake could swallow the pig's head first. The python already boasted a large diameter, but as the pig was devoured, it formed a grotesque bulge in the snake's body. Because there was no blood, the death almost seemed civilized and yet, a most horrifying sight.

I tried to pull Mateo away. We'd been watching for a long time.

"Kill it." He kept saying. "We could eat it."

I didn't argue. Instead, I handed Mateo the knife. "Pythons usually release their prey if found while eating because they are helpless at this time. So, he must be starving to eat while we are watching."

Mateo looked at the knife now in his hand, then glanced up at me and said, "I have a bird's nest.

Let's go build a fire." We left the snake and headed toward the firepit. "You know that we will have to haul the boat up into a tree for the night. I will not sleep on the ground after seeing that."

I laughed, not only thinking about trying to pull a boat up into a tree but more because of Mateo's girly scream. I better not mention that last part…ever.

The nest caught on fire right away. I added a few of the small pieces of wood I had chopped earlier. They made tiny coals that burned away any moisture in the sticks we slowly piled on top.

I dropped a larger piece of wood near the small flame to dry before putting it on the tiny coals. "Don't worry about that snake. It won't eat again for weeks."

Mateo's eyebrows arched. "I will not sleep on the ground."

"How are we going to move the boat with tree limbs in front of it? And even if you did get the boat out from under all that brush, how would you get it up a tree?"

"I'll think about how while we bake our fish."

Black clouds once again stormed our way. We could hear the deep rumbles of thunder but stayed right where we were, hoping to finish cooking our dinner. The wind kicked up, and it started to sprinkle. Lightning lit the sky, but we stayed at the fire, not worrying about the sparks igniting the woods. We had learned that the rain would take care of our small fire in no time at all.

A lightning strike close by made me very uncomfortable, and even though the fish might not be done all the way, I took my stick of fish and fled toward the boat. I crawled through the branches and sat on the log.

I sprayed bug repellent on a big brown spider and me. I watched the spider scurry off. Mateo joined me, so I handed him the can of spray and started to eat. The normal routine of washing your hands before dinner had gotten suspended. A swim, fully clothed, would have to happen in the morning as I could smell myself and my friend. I was sure that my appearance would shock people and make everyone think of me as a homeless beggar.

This storm wasn't as bad as the tempest this morning and simmered down to a sprinkle while we finished eating the fish. I made my way to get a drink and heard the birds singing. That told me the storm was over, at least for now.

After Mateo drank his fill, we crawled out to see if we could fix the fire, but everything had gotten soaked. A crashing in the woods sent me back under the boat to grab our walking sticks.

Three wild hogs ran into the clearing close to the python: one big male, a medium-sized female, and a baby. I would guess they searched for the other baby. Then they saw us.

Mateo whispered, "Move slowly and get under the boat."

Surprisingly they did not follow, but that was the end of staying on the ground for both of us. We'd seen and dealt with enough drama for one day and decided we would climb and stay in a tree overnight once the pigs vacated the area. I left my camera under the boat on the makeshift shelf.

"Grab a towel and tuck it in the waist of your pants, and I'll do the same. We'll climb the tree by the clearing. It's big and branchy enough to hold us both. We'll have to take our sticks with us."

"What if a boat comes by? The clearing is too far from the water."

"You worry too much."

"Pythons can climb trees," I said.

"I know." Mateo held up his stick "We can beat it down with these, and I promise not to fall asleep on my watch."

The hogs must not have found the python because they soon left. The sun had not set, but Mateo wanted to climb the tree now, before dusk.

He laced his stick between several branches and then leaned back against the bracing. "Now I can relax."

"Do you hear that?" I straightened and concentrated on the sound. "Is that a motor?"

"Couldn't be. Not in this weather."

But it was *Emmie*. She drove right up and paused a moment surveying the damage, I suppose.

We bellowed her name over and over, but she couldn't hear us over the airboat motor.

I scrambled down, falling out of the tree. Trying to catch Emmie before she left was impossible. She was gone before I'd made it to the edge of the water. If only we had been on the ground, or if I would have gotten out of the tree sooner, I might have caught her.

I stood and stared at the river.

Mateo threw his stick and screamed at me, "Are you going to cry?"

The sensation of failure morphed into rage. I raised my face toward Mateo, and said in an icy voice, "At least, I don't scream like a girl when I see a snake."

CHAPTER FOURTEEN

Night 2

After Emmie drove away and my anger toward Mateo's meanness faded, we both stayed silent. Mateo must have been tired because I heard a snore every once in a while.

I sat on a fallen tree, longing for pen and paper to write about my experiences in the Everglades. Instead, I made mental notes and studied the area. Plant life thrived there. *The pictures I had taken were now priceless.*

Danger lurked everywhere, and yet the beauty of the glades was undeniable. Bugs and mosquitoes drove me crazy. They didn't bother so much when we had the fire, but now with the bug spray gone, there was nothing to keep them away. Mud helped.

I crawled under the boat, thinking that I might spend the night there, alone, away from Mateo. I resented that he brought up that I had cried. He thought he was so tough, but I shouldn't have said anything about his scream. He probably didn't know that he screamed like a girl. The thought made me chuckle.

Staying on a piece of land in the middle of nowhere and living through a huge thunderstorm proved to be the hardest time in my life. The hope of Emmie coming back in the morning might be the best help to get through the night.

She must not have been able to tell we were here, or she wouldn't have driven away. I pictured what she would have seen. Was there any clue that we were here? She would not have been able to see the boat or the motor behind the mangrove leaves. There was nothing for her to see from the water except the destruction of a place she loved. She was probably heartbroken.

Mateo called out to me. Part of me wanted to stay right where I was, but the towel I used to keep the mosquitoes at bay was in the tree. The night surrounded me, and with the darkness came the creepy sounds of the wild. I crawled out through the branches. It freaked me out because I couldn't see much, and even when I stood, my path was barely visible.

"Hey, where are you?" he called out. "I think you should come up here with me."

"I'm coming, but I can't see. Would you keep talking?"

"Well, that's awkward, but okay. The storm today was badass. Good thing we weren't here in hurricane season."

"December through April is supposed to be dry, or at least, that's what I read somewhere."

"From the sound of your voice, I can tell that you're almost here. I've got your stick braced behind where you sit. It makes sitting on a limb almost comfortable. There are fewer mosquitoes, maybe because of the bats."

As I made my way up the tree, I asked, "Do you think Emmie will come back here tomorrow?"

"I was wondering that, too. She doesn't know that we're here. We might be on our own for another day or two. We've done okay on our own. We have plenty of water now and can catch food."

"Right. We should be okay until the python gets hungry." I laughed even though that wasn't funny. I was sure there were more super snakes out there. Another silence between us, but this time, it wasn't uncomfortable.

"One good thing will come of this." Mateo paused, and I wondered what the good thing could be. "You'll have one heck of a story to write," he finished.

I had to laugh at how right he was. "It would be a good article, but I'm not so sure I could capture the true horror of being out here for days."

Mateo leaned toward me, and even though I couldn't see his face, I knew the way his eyebrows arched at that moment. "Are you kidding me? I don't like to read, but I read your story about the rodeo. You're a great writer. Your details made it real. Everyone talked about that story for days."

"An editor I met on the cruise asked me to send the rodeo article to a magazine here in Miami, so I did. They rejected the piece. The real writers, publishers, and editors could tell that I'm not a real writer."

"Are you going to cry?" Mateo asked, then laughed…a lot.

After pouring my heart out, I couldn't understand how it was funny to slam me. I should have stayed under the boat. I stood up, getting ready to go.

"Don't go. I was kidding. It was a mean thing to say, but really, I was kidding. I thought that would be funny, so you'd stop feeling sorry for yourself."

"It wasn't funny, and I don't feel sorry for myself." The minute those words left my mouth, shame entered. *I am feeling sorry for myself.*

"Mitchell, everyone loved that story. The whole rodeo circuit read and liked the story. Maybe you should find out why the magazine rejected it, especially after you were asked to send it to them."

"The standard form letter wasn't personal and didn't say why. I'd feel stupid questioning a national magazine." *Maybe he was right.* I should fight for what I want. At least find out why, so I can better myself.

"Whether you ask them or not, you have to write about this adventure. So much has happened to us. You'll have to write a short story or a book."

"I brought my phone up here with me. I don't mean to be a pessimist, but what if Emmie never returns? I know my dad will have called the police or someone by now. If I turn my phone on, even for just a few minutes, I think it will show that we are here."

Mateo made a sound like he wasn't sure. "Even if you don't have service? Why don't you try calling 911? You never know. It's worth a try."

I tried, but it didn't work. *He might be right about not creating a ping if you don't have service.*

We got quiet. An owl seemed to be trying to outdo the frogs. After a while, all their noise turned into background static. The rain clouds moved north, leaving an open sky with millions of twinkling stars.

Mateo snored softly, so I knew it was my watch. The night danger seemed less while we were in the tree. My walking stick was right behind me in case a snake attempted to climb our tree. All in all, we were safe, so I dozed off and on throughout the night, letting Mateo sleep.

CHAPTER FIFTEEN

Day 3

Mateo woke me. "I'm going to look for food. You get a bit more sleep. I know you kept watch last night, so finding breakfast will be my thank you." He handed me his lighter.

How did he expect me to sleep when he just gave me a job?

He scrambled down from the tree. I expected him to head to the river, but he went through the clearing and into the woods. He didn't take the pole to catch iguana, so I couldn't be sure what he would bring back.

Sleep time was over, and a new day began with the hope of rescue. Would Emmie notice that Steve's truck and boat were gone? Why wasn't she at work yesterday? I gathered small twigs and dead grass to start a fire. We would need the hot coals for cooking and to keep mosquitoes away, plus something about the fire made me feel better.

The flame caught right away. I added twigs and then sticks, and the blaze grew with the addition of more fuel. Every time I reached to put wood in the fire, I caught a whiff of myself. *No more putting off a bath.* After breakfast, our next adventure would be a swim with the gators.

If Emmie didn't come today, we would have to hunt for iguana, catch fishing, or something. It seemed like all we did was gather wood, hunt for food, eat, and sleep. In all my research of the Everglades, I never studied what roots or greens you could safely eat. I never imagined we would be stuck out here. *Not a good time for trial and error in what not to eat.*

Mateo walked toward the fire holding the bottom of his shirt to make a pouch. "Look what I found. He held the shirt out to show me four nice-sized, brown speckled eggs.

"I think those are osprey eggs. How'd you get them?"

They had a big nest built in the top of a tree back there." Mateo pointed in the direction of the woods.

"You're lucky that the parents didn't catch you. Ospreys are from the raptor family. You know, sharp talons, hooked beak, and an attitude." My mind flashed pictures of that old dinosaur movie. "How will we cook them?"

"I'm drinking my two."

My stomach lurched at the thought of slurping down a raw egg. My face must have shown my thoughts.

"Eat it or go hungry. Your choice." Then Mateo cracked, opened, and sucked down an egg. "Not too bad. I'm getting my last soda. Want yours?"

I nodded, then held my hand out for an egg. I didn't want to try this, but my stomach spoke hunger. I cracked and opened it, but smelled first. *No odor.* I stuck my tongue on it. Slimy. That was a stupid thing to do. I had to eat, so I just downed it, then held out my hand for the other one. Having something in my stomach made me feel better, but I hoped we would find a tastier treat for dinner.

Mateo laughed and ate his second one. We stayed by the fire, joked about drinking raw eggs, and then spoke of the hope that Emmie would come soon. "I'll bet we could talk her into taking us to McDonald's for lunch."

"Let's get cleaned up. It will be dangerous to take a swim, but the smell will kill me if we don't." I got up, hoping he would, too.

"Good idea. I'm going to wash my clothes and hang them on a tree to dry," Mateo said. "We'll have to watch for gators and snakes, so it will be safer if we stand back-to-back."

I put a couple more chunks of wood in the pit, and we left for the river. I didn't see any critters, so I hung my towel in a tree, stripped, got waist-deep in the water using my clothes to wash my body, and then scrubbed the clothes. I dunked my head underwater, swishing my clothes over my face and hair.

We were both covered in bug bites, some scabbed over from scratching them. The bugs were the worst in the morning and the evening. They must not like the sun, smoke, or treetops.

After getting out, we hung our clothes in the downed tree branches and headed to the fire to get warm and escape more bug bites.

Mateo threw more wood on the fire and noted that we would have to gather more. "Do you hear the sound of a motor?"

We ran to the water's edge and glanced in each direction. The sound faded. Neither of us cared that we only had towels to cover our nakedness.

"Even if we had screamed our guts out, they wouldn't hear us over their boat motors. We should start making oars and not just leave our future to chance." Mateo tightened his towel around his waist and turned away.

"I don't mean to change the subject, Mateo, but did you just see that baby alligator? Look, there's a bunch of them. We'd better get out of here. I'm sure that the mom is close."

"Gator meat is good. That's what we should have for supper." Mateo grabbed his clothes. "I don't care if they are all the way dry. I'm gonna catch a bunch of these young gators."

Mateo used the pole that was set up with a lasso. I kept the fire going then watched Mateo's speed and skill. Those young gators didn't have a chance. He killed each one as he caught it so they couldn't call out for their mom, and we never saw her. Maybe our luck was changing.

With six gators, each about a foot long, we headed to the fire. Mateo took his knife and cut through the outer skin. You couldn't peel the skin like on a rabbit or iguana. He had to pull the hide and slice it away from the body inch by inch.

While he worked, I fed the fire and took pictures. "You know Emmie will be working all week. It's only Wednesday. She said that she brings Violet out here on Sundays." I handed him another gator to skin, took the meat from the one he'd just finished, and laid it in the glowing red coals. I was surprised at how much meat a gator offered.

Mateo didn't say anything about being here until Sunday. What could he say?

"You are right about figuring our way out of here. After we cook this meat, let's get busy making oars. I don't know why I didn't think of that."

"Another reason your dad chose me for this trip." Mateo had to rub it in.

CHAPTER SIXTEEN

Lubber

I'd never eaten fire-roasted gator or any gator, and it smelled good.

Mateo placed the meat in a towel. "I'll hold both ends of the towel over the sides of the chest, stretched tight enough to keep the meat out of the water, and then you shut the lid."

"Mateo, is that towel the one you used or mine?" He didn't answer my question.

"We have to find an oar length piece of wood. It might take a while to flatten the end, but I know we can do this." Mateo's face showed determination. "We should gather firewood while we hunt for the oar wood." He laughed at his weird wood wording.

"Take your walking stick. No telling what we'll find in our search." I took off, heading into the woods but toward the river. We had used up most of the dead sticks around our camp, so I went deeper into the trees, watching my surroundings so I wouldn't get lost.

The most beautiful grasshopper posed on a log for a picture. I squatted beside him and stared at the bright yellow and orange with black patterns on his body. His rear legs attached to the body and rose a couple of inches to a knee joint, then down to the log. I would guess he could make long jumps with those legs.

It seemed strange that he didn't jump, just stared back at me with big black eyes. I would guess that the body of this guy measured about three or four inches long. I picked up the log, holding it so he wouldn't fall off, and carried it to the camp.

Mateo had just dropped some wood near the pit. "What do you have?"

"Check out this giant grasshopper. I know I've seen pictures of them, but I can't remember the name of it."

"Do you think they are poisonous?"

Before I had time to answer, he had put his hand by its face, and the grasshopper crawled onto his outstretched hand. We studied it for a few minutes, and then it jumped. Those long back legs did aid in his long jump into the bushes.

"Lubber." I suddenly remembered. "It's called a Lubber Grasshopper, and it isn't poisonous." I headed into the woods and found more wood for the fire. How would we find a piece of wood with a wide end? Impossible. I dropped the firewood by the pit and started toward the water.

Mateo called out, "Look what I found." He carried a huge turtle.

"Are we going to eat it?" But as he got closer, I could see there was no turtle in the shell. "Wow, that's huge.

"I thought you'd like to see it. Wonder if it burns. We could use it like coal."

"Or a paddle." Pride of my sharp thinking must have shown on my face.

Mateo had a blank expression like he was thinking.

"We could wedge a stick into it and use it as an oar."

"Maybe. But what if it fell off halfway back? Maybe we could wedge the wood in and tie it with vines. Using the shell for a paddle is a good idea, Mitchell."

"What if we got a couple of long sticks and used one as a pole in the shallow places and the turtle paddle in the deeper waters?

"Let's think about that while we finish getting firewood." Mateo headed into the woods.

We worked until the sunset turned the sky red and purple with yellow streaks. The amount of wood we'd gathered would easily last a couple of days. With any luck, that was all we would need. Mateo built a fire, and then we climbed through the branches to get our gator meat.

The fire roared, but we'd have to wait for hot coals before warming up the meat. Night settled in around us, and we found our sitting spots.

"We had a bonfire every night at the rodeos. My family and I would sit around the fire just like we are now. Most of the talk centered around the animals, the funny or scary things that had happened that day, or strategy for the next day's events. I miss my family." Mateo went on talking about bull riding, roping, and all the places he'd been.

When the subject came around to me and my writing, I told him about my muse. "The muse is not a spirit like some people think. I believe it is the subconscious part of the brain, giving you twists and turns for the story. It's like someone whispering ideas in your head. I write all the ideas down into a plot that I can follow. The funny thing is that just when you think you know the story, then the muse makes changes. That's what I love."

"Sounds like a lot of work, but I can see that you enjoy that type of thing."

The sweet smell of roasted gator made my mouth water and made me think of home, for some strange reason. "My mom is sick. I don't think the doctors are right about her having asthma or bronchitis. I'm afraid there's something seriously wrong with her lungs. I don't know what Dad or I would do without her. She can be amazingly irritating, like when we were planning this trip. She decided we would stay in Miami."

"In Miami, you would have had a pool and meals served." Mateo grinned. "But this is so much better."

We both got a good laugh and ate the gator. I wished we had salt, but we both enjoyed the meal. The sun had disappeared completely, and the sky sparkled with a million stars. I stared at the sky in wonder.

"Should we stay right here and sleep by the fire tonight?" Mateo asked.

"Do you think we'd be safe from the pythons?" It wasn't long after those words that I fell asleep.

He must have slept, too, because when I awoke, the pit had nothing but glowing coals.

Mateo tossed a stick at me. "Our families are going to call us men of adventure. My dad already thinks you are very brave."

"Me?"

"Everyone loves you for saving those horses from being burned alive in the barn fire."

"I had to ride Molly to lead the bronco out. He was frantic with fear. You would have done the same thing." I heard rustling on the ground and saw a blur of motion run across the clearing. "Did you see that?"

CHAPTER SEVENTEEN

Panther

"Yes, I saw that panther, and hope he was only passing through." Mateo grabbed his stuff and headed to the tree.

We made it up the tree quickly, even though we carried our sticks and towels. I braced my stick in the branches, but instead of leaning against it, I leaned into it. This angle gave me a better view. I wanted to catch sight of the big cat again, but the woods went quiet. Too quiet.

I dreamed, or rather I should say, had a nightmare that someone tried to pull me out of the tree. I couldn't see their face, only knew that they kept tugging at my dangling foot. Then pain. Real pain. I opened my eyes and turned to see the black-lined eyes of the panther. He had my foot in his mouth and yanked again to dislodge me from my perch.

Thank God that I had leaned into the braced walking stick so the panther couldn't pull me off. That cat would have pulled me through the branch that I sat on, but still, it had a good hold on my ankle and foot and wouldn't let go. I could feel my flesh tearing and screamed.

Mateo must have been awakened by the thrashing around because, just as I screamed, he stood on a limb, pulled his stick from the branches, and with brute force, poked that cat square in the eye.

The hurt and angry animal dropped to the ground, only to leap onto the limb below us. The panther did not intend to give up. Blood poured from its eye.

Mateo, still standing on the branch, took a stance, held his arms out to his sides while holding his stick, and roared a giant unreal sound that frightened the cat enough to jump to the ground.

My foot hurt, but in the dark, it was hard to see. I pulled my leg up to rest on the branch next to me so that I could get a better look. I pulled up my wet pant leg to see a large gash and a dark circle, where his eye tooth must have punctured for holding power. I was losing a lot of blood and already felt light-headed and weak.

Mateo roared again. He gave the impression of being a big, bad monster that could eat the nasty animal in one bite. The cat stayed right under the tree, staring at us…waiting.

My friend came around the tree and balanced, so he could lean forward, far enough, to get a good look at my wound.

"Can you pull the towel out from under you? Never mind, I'll get mine." He wasn't gone long. Taking out his knife, he cut and ripped a strip from the length of the towel. "Here, slide this under your leg, just under the knee."

While I did as he said, Mateo made guttural noises and smacked his stick on the tree to warn the, now standing, panther. It stayed and continued to stare, while Mateo turned his attention to my leg.

He pulled and cut a small branch from the tree and then handed it to me. "Tie another loop around this stick, knot it, and twist to tighten. It will cut off the flow of blood."

I did what he told me. The pain dulled into a throbbing ache. The flow of blood lessened.

"Now, I want you to raise your leg to the branch just above the one you're sitting on. It won't be comfortable until I figure a way to support your back, but you have to do this." Mateo spoke with an authority I'd never heard before from anyone, not even my mom.

He pulled at the smaller branches above us, cutting and weaving them. I watched Mateo make something that looked like a chair back, then he ripped three strips from the towel, tying the brace right behind me so that I could relax with my leg up. *Genius.*

I was sure he'd never been in a situation like this before, but you would never have known it. Instantaneously, he thought of what to do and then did it like he'd done it a hundred times before. He also kept an eye on the panther, and every time it twitched, Mateo would go into combat mode, keeping the big cat at bay.

The golden sunrise promised a beautiful day, but that was a lie because this day might be my last. *How long can I keep a tourniquet on before it kills the part of my body that's not getting blood flow?* How long would the cat stay there, waiting for us to make a mistake, fall asleep, or become too weak from dehydration?

Mateo must have read my mind. "Don't worry. We'll be all right. See that vine up there?" He pointed toward the upper part of the tree. "That's one of those climbers that carries water."

He scampered up the tree like an anxious squirrel, stopping every few feet, I think, to check on my safety. The fear that coursed through my body when Mateo left almost made me physically ill. I had no protection and doubted that Mateo would be able to make it back before I would be torn to pieces. I'd never thought of myself as a coward until now.

Weird, but the cat laid down and pawed its face. Of course, his eye hurt, probably worse than my leg. I wished my camera was with me, but I'd left it under the boat.

****

After what seemed a long time, Mateo handed me a piece of vine. "Suck and chew on this. We could even try swallowing the fibers after chewing it into pulp."

I didn't want to tell him my fears of not making it out of the Everglades, so I tried to make a joke. "Is this another reason my dad chose you to come with me?"

He didn't laugh.

Mateo's watery eyes showed the beginning of a smile. "You have to admit, your dad made a good choice."

I laughed because it was so true. "Dude, you should have seen yourself when you stood on that branch and roared at that cat."

"I told the panther I was going to kill it. Look at him. That panther knows to be afraid because he knows what I said. And I will kill him if I have to."

CHAPTER EIGHTEEN

Emmie Enlightened

The sounds of a Thursday morning in Miami woke me. I thought about my dream, or was it a remembrance? Visions of the horrible damage in the glades plagued me, and I couldn't stop thinking about seeing a campfire pit. I tried to remember if I had seen a fire pit when I was out there on Tuesday. I wasn't sure. But If I did, then the boys must have been there because I never had a fire there.

After pouring a cup of coffee, I called the office. "Hi Karen, I'm not coming in today, there's something I have to do. Remember those boys I told you about? Well, they may be camped out in the Everglades."

"We should have Christmas Eve off anyway." She agreed. "Have a great weekend, and I'll see you next week."

How would those boys have gotten out there, and when? I hurried with those thoughts in mind. The drive to Homestead didn't take long. My first stop was to be the marina, but instead, I drove past Steve's, hoping to see the boys.

The police, Steve, and other men, I'd never seen before, all stood in the front yard. I did not see the boys. I pulled up and parked behind one of the police cars, and then walked across the street to find out what was happening.

One of the cops stood near the road. I approached him. "Officer, my name is Emmie." I noticed his name badge read Patin. "My grandmother, Violet Cardy, lives a couple of blocks over." I pointed in the direction of my grandmother's house and then continued, "I stopped because I'm worried about two boys who were staying here."

"Emmie, when did you last see them?"

"Last Sunday, Mitchell and Mateo helped my grandmother board the windows at her house. For a thank you, I took them on an airboat ride. Are they all right?"

"Mitchell and Mateo's dads are here. Would you mind talking with them?"

I nodded. "I don't mind talking to them." We crossed the yard to join the others.

Officer Patin quietly spoke to his partner for a few minutes then introduced me, telling the men how I knew their sons. Both of the dads fired off questions, but Steve's was the loudest, "Emmie, where are my truck and boat?"

I had never noticed the truck missing. "Steve, I can't answer that for sure, but I would guess the Everglades." Then I told them everything I knew, even about my ride in the glades after the storm on Tuesday. "The place I had taken the guys to on Sunday had big trees down." I took a deep breath. "Last night, I had a dream that makes me think they might be out there."

Officer Patin said, "They left a note on the table saying that they were headed for the Everglades. We all know it's a big place. Emmie, what makes you think they went to the same place you had taken them on Sunday?"

I glanced up, gathering my courage. "I dreamed about seeing a firepit. There's never been a firepit there, so if it's just a dream, then the boys may not be there. They wanted to go fishing, and they know that is a great fishing hole. I believe that it's a good place to start the search."

The taller of the two dads spoke. "Emmie, I'm Roger Lavender. My son is Mitchell. This is Miguel Lopez, Mateo's dad. Could you take us to that place now?"

"Absolutely."

Officer Patin said, "I'd like to go with you. Do you have enough seating for four?"

I nodded.

"Sam, I'll give you a call when we get back or let you know if we need to expand the search."

When we passed the boat launch, I noticed Steve's truck and pointed it out. Guilt and regret of not paying attention made me cringe. I should have noticed days ago that the truck was gone from the house. At the marina, I parked, and it only took minutes to get on our way.

Driving three men through the everglades seemed strange, yet made me feel proud because I was the captain of the boat. Mr. Lavender and Mr. Lopez's faces showed worry. They sat in front of Officer Patin and me.

I slowed as we reached our destination, and a smile covered my face. There was a firepit. But just as quickly, the smile faded. That meant that those boys had been out here for four days. I drove up on land just enough so the men didn't have to get wet.

Officer Patin pointed at the campfire and mouthed, "A fire pit, but no boat."

I shut the motor down.

We could hear the guys in the distance. The sound seemed a long way off, but they must see us. I scanned the area but couldn't find them.

Mr. Lopez pointed up. "There they are."

We all ran in that direction until Mateo screamed, "Stop. There's a panther."

We stood behind Officer Patin, who had pulled his gun.

Mateo, still standing on a branch high above, glanced toward the woods. "You scared the panther, but we can't trust that he won't come back."

Both men shouted greetings to their sons.

"Hurry, Mitchell is hurt and bleeding bad."

Mr. Lavender rushed ahead and climbed the tree.

Mr. Lopez stayed on the ground near the base of the tree, while Mateo stayed with Mitchell to help get him down.

Still ravaged with guilt, I stood next to the policeman, who watched for the panther.

"Can you get him down?" Officer Patin hollered.

"I believe so." Mr. Lavender lifted Mitchell to a stand. "He's a tough kid." They took one branch at a time. Mateo would go down to steady Mitchell's body until Mr. Lavender would get past them and do the same. It was a slow process until they reached the last branch.

Officer Patin and Mr. Lopez then lowered Mitchell from the tree and carried him to the boat.

Mateo came right to me and gave me a huge hug. "I knew you'd come back eventually."

"I'm so sorry. Where were you when I came on Tuesday?"

"We climbed the tree after watching a python eat a baby pig. The panther found us last night while we were sleeping." Mateo's last few words sounded thick, but he continued, "Mitchell's leg is pretty bad."

I stepped closer and looped my arm around his waist.

Mateo jerked and ran to the mass of leaves covering Steve's boat. "I've got to get Mitchell's phone and camera."

Officer Patin spoke into his phone, calling for an ambulance to meet us at the marina. Then turned his attention to the rest of us. "Let's go. This boy needs to get to the hospital."

Mateo walked toward us, holding up Mitchell's phone. "Mitchell couldn't get service out here."

Officer Patin held up his phone and said, "Satellite."

The boys sat on the floor directly in front of their dad. Mr. Lavender examined Mitchell's leg.

"We're overloaded, but I'll go slow. I'm sorry you're hurt, Mitchell. I didn't know you guys were here until I woke up this morning, thinking I had seen a firepit. I still didn't know for sure until we got here."

Mitchell twisted around to look at me. "Emmie, I've never been so grateful to anyone. Thank you for bringing my dad." I could tell from his eyes that he was in a lot of pain.

Officer Patin asked, "Where's the boat?"

Both boys pointed at the downed tree. "The boat is okay, but it's behind all that brush.

Officer Patin took the seat next to me. "All right, you boys, hang on to your dads' legs. Let's go, Emmie."

I started the engine and tried to be smooth but had to gun it to get into the water. We jerked to start, and I could see that Mitchell's leg started to bleed. My focus had to stay on getting us all home safely. Once in the water, the ride smoothed out, and everyone relaxed a little.

The glades appeared to have had a tornado thunder through, or maybe straight-line winds. Part of me worried about the wildlife, but another part knew they were used to the ups and downs life threw at them.

The red flashing lights of the ambulance with a police car right beside it made for a welcome sight. The paramedics met us at the water's edge with a portable gurney. When they put Mitchell on the stretcher, I saw his leg, and my stomach roiled.

Mr. Lavender got in the ambulance after they loaded Mitchell.

Mr. Lopez turned to me. "Are you going to go to the hospital?"

I nodded as the urge to throw up made speaking impossible. *This was all my fault.*

Mr. Lopez ran to the ambulance, had a quick word with Mr. Lavender, and then made his way back to stand near Mateo and me. "Would it be okay if Mateo and I rode to the hospital with you?"

Before I could answer, I ran to a tree by the water and threw up. By the time I returned, the ambulance and police had gone, and the marine service guys had taken care of my boat.

Mr. Lopez asked for my keys, and he drove. Mateo stayed right by my side.

"I'd like to pick up my grandma before we go to the hospital." I directed my words to Mr. Lopez.

But Mateo answered, "Only if we can stop at the first fast food we find."

CHAPTER NINETEEN

Hospital

Emmie

I gave Mr. Lopez directions to Gram's house while we waited for Mateo's food and had myself under control, but the minute we pulled into the driveway, my tears fell. My grandmother would understand how I felt.

Gram opened the front door and took a few steps into the yard before I reached her and melted into her open arms.

"Emmie, what happened?" Gram held me at arms-length, searching my eyes then pulling me in for another hug. "Mateo, you're safe. Where's Mitchell?"

Mateo put his hand on my shoulder. "Yes, I'm safe, thanks to Emmie, and Mitchell is safe now, too. I think your granddaughter feels responsible for what Mitchell and I did, which is not true." He held my gaze for a moment and then turned to Gram. "We took Steve's boat to the Everglades and got stuck out there for days. Not her fault. Did you hear me, Emmie? Not your fault."

Mr. Lopez, still by the truck, introduced himself and then said, "Mitchell is at the hospital with a panther bite to his leg. We should go there, soon."

I took a deep breath, pulled away from Gram, and asked, "Would you like to go with us?"

Gram didn't answer for a minute then said, "The Wilson's are here, so how about I make a big dinner? You all come here to eat after you visit Mitchell. I would like to hear the details of staying in the Everglades with no provisions."

"They went out there Monday," I said.

Mateo proudly grinned.

Mr. Lopez said, "We would be grateful for your hospitality."

****

Mitchell

"Mitchell, please lay down, at least until we get in there." Dad's jaw twitched, and he gave me the stare-down.

The EMT guys seemed like being bit by a panther was pretty serious, and they couldn't believe the cat stayed after being poked in the eye. I noticed the somber grimace they exchanged. We entered the emergency section of the hospital.

Christmas decorations at the nurse's station gave a sense of comfort. The paramedics turned me over to the nurse, who hurried me into a curtained-off area. A male nurse came in, and the two moved me from the wheeled gurney onto a hospital bed.

After they left, Dad asked, "How awful was it in the Everglades for three nights?"

"Sometimes hard, like finding food. Sometimes fun, like sitting around the fire looking at the stars and talking about our families. Sometimes terrifying, like taking cover under a boat during a huge storm." I turned my head to see Dad's face. He seemed so sad.

"Dad, you know how Grandma talks about Divine intervention? Well, that happened to me. When we were in the tree, I braced my walking stick behind me and leaned against it. But last night, I turned around for no real reason. If I hadn't turned around, the panther would have pulled me right out of the tree."

Before Dad had time to respond, the doctor opened the curtain.

He stood there for a minute, then introduced himself, "I'm Doctor Frank Yates, better known as Doc. You're my first patient today with a panther bite. Or did they get that wrong?"

"That's true. A panther bit me. Are panther bites rare?" I suddenly felt embarrassed about my appearance when I noticed how dirty and tattered my clothes were and how carefully dressed and groomed my dad and the doc appeared.

"Panther bites are rare. I was being facetious." He examined my leg and said, "Tell me what happened."

"A friend and I have been in the Everglades since Monday. We were sleeping in a tree because of a giant python." I noticed my dad straighten up and lean toward me. I hadn't told him that part. "During the night, a panther tried to jerk me out of the tree."

"A panther attacking a human is rare. Maybe that cat saw your dangling leg and decided to have some fun. But the reason for the attack could be more serious. The paramedics said your friend stabbed the panther in the eye, and yet it stayed. I'm wondering if the animal is diseased. There will be no way to tell without having access to the cat."

My dad stood and said, "Are you thinking rabies?" Dad's face was white, and he looked like he might pass out.

"Yes, the panther might have been infected. We're going to assume by all the signs that it did carry rabies. We'll clean the wound again, start IV antibiotics, stitch him up, and begin the rabies treatment."

"Are you saying he will be admitted?" Dad took a seat.

"I'd like to keep him overnight to start."

"How do you treat rabies?" I asked.

"You will get a shot after we clean the wound, then a series of shots over fourteen-days."

My expression must have mirrored my feelings because the doctor quickly continued, "You will receive four shots in total. Today will be the first, then the third day, the seventh day, and the fourteenth day. What is your pain level on a scale from one to ten, right now?"

"About a six."

"I'll be back in the morning. It was nice to meet you both." The doctor left the room.

Seconds later, a nurse came in with a bag of liquid that she hung from a pole and then put a needle in my arm, taped it down, and started the IV. "The tubing will not only be used to hydrate your body but will also be used to administer the antibiotics." She held up a syringe. "This medicine will help with the pain." She put the needle into a joint in the tubing.

"You have some visitors, but only for a few minutes while the medication takes effect." As she left, she wiggled her index finger like a warning to behave.

Mateo, Emmie, and Miguel peeked around the curtain. Dad laughed then invited them in. They put a bag of food and a coke on the table beside me.

"Oh man, thank you!" I took a drink of soda. "I have to be treated for rabies. I will get four injections over 14 days."

"You have to stay here for two weeks?" Mateo blurted out.

"No, just overnight."

Dad corrected my wording. "The doctor said overnight to start. I'm sure he will assess the situation tomorrow and make a decision." Dad pointed at my phone. "If you'd like, I can take it with me and get it charged."

"That would be wonderful. I've missed having it for a hundred reasons." I handed Dad the phone and watched as he tucked it in his jacket.

"Gram is making a big dinner for us. Do you want us to sneak you up some dessert?" Emmie asked.

"You bet, I'm starving, and I've had your grandmother's cookies. They were excellent. I'm looking forward to eating more than iguana, fish, and gator." I loved the surprised look on Emmie's face about what we had been eating, and I took a bite of the juicy burger.

The nurse came in with a tray, set it on the desk, and lifted another syringe. "I'm sorry, but this one goes in your arm for tetanus. You have a few more minutes to visit." Before she left, I was already feeling groggy from the pain meds.

"Dad, when are you and Mr. Lopez returning to Michigan?"

"We didn't purchase return tickets because we didn't know what to expect when we got here. We hadn't heard from either of you boys in days. But to answer your question, we will all be leaving at the same time. It will depend on how long you have to stay here."

"We haven't even been here a week," I lamented. "Did you get my stuff at Steve's?"

"Not yet," Dad said. "I'm sure he wants your things out of his house. He's not a very nice man, but you can't blame him."

Mr. Lopez took a step forward. "I don't think we got the whole story from Steve. He told us the boys stole the boat, but earlier, he told Mateo that if they fixed the motor, they could take the boat."

I didn't want to go home yet. I wanted to go to Miami and talk to my friend, David O'Brien, at the magazine. I longed for time to go to the library and write, while everything was fresh in my head – not just any library but one near the Everglades.

Mateo must have read my mind. "Mitchell wanted to go to some big magazine publisher in Miami and talk about the story he'd sent them and tell them about what happened to us. Will he still be able to do that?"

Mr. Lopez answered, "Like Roger already said, we didn't know what to plan when we came, but I think we should go tomorrow night or Saturday morning. That means you, boys, too."

"Mitchell can write or call Mr. O'Brien from home," Dad said. "I'm sure my wife and your family want us to come home for a late Christmas celebration."

Mr. Lopez nodded and said, "Our family is holding off opening presents, and you know how serious that is, Mateo."

We all had a chuckle about that.

Emmie had been silent until now. "Maybe the boys could come back after Christmas and stay with me in Miami, go to the magazine, and visit Miami Zoo to see the Everglade Exhibit. Gram would have to stay with us, too. Otherwise, the neighbors might get the wrong idea. I have some vacation time I could use."

CHAPTER TWENTY

Arizona

People spoke in whispers. I opened my eyes and found myself in a hospital room with a big piece of chocolate cake and my phone on the hospital table in front of me. Dad stood in the middle of the room, talking to the kid in the next bed. "Merry Christmas."

I didn't even realize that was today. "Merry Christmas," I replied, sat upright, and reached for the cake. "Where is everyone?" Then turned on my phone.

"You were asleep, so we figured you'd be out for the rest of the night. We were all tired and full after leaving Violet's house. Mateo showered, changed, and got into bed as soon as he got into the hotel room. He and his dad were watching some cop show when I left for my room."

"This cake is so moist and chocolaty." I used a tissue to wipe off my upper lip. "Dad, what do you think of Emmie's offer of Mateo and I staying with her?"

Dad pulled the curtain, and he wasn't smiling. "I think you made some wonderful friends. Better than the people I had you hooked up with, but Emmie feels responsible for your disastrous trip."

"She didn't have anything to do with us going into the Everglades on our own. Dad, I'm pretty sure I know you're going to say no, and I get it." We were both quiet for a few minutes, then I asked, "How's Mom? It's easy to tell there is more going on than what I've been told."

He walked around the bed to a chair. His shoulders drooped and he appeared to be praying or in deep thought. Long minutes passed. In a very soft voice, he said, "I think you're right, but she's had numerous tests, and we still don't know."

"Who is staying with Mom right now?"

"Your grandmother is staying at our house while I'm here with you. Both of those ladies are worried about you, not to mention your friends. Andy brought Haylee to the house a few days ago so she could talk to your mom."

Holding my phone up, I said, "You should see how many times those two have called me."

The doctor pulled the curtain back and stepped closer. "I've got good news. You're going to stay with us another night." He smiled, but I didn't.

Dad stood even straighter than he usually does. "Is there a problem?"

"Not really. The nurses tell me that Mitchell had a good night's sleep and everything appears all right. I'm being cautious and would like to observe him one more night. Rabies is very serious, and in some cases can be a deadly disease."

I cleared my throat before making a statement that would surprise my dad. "My mom is not well, and I'd like to go home as soon as I can. Would that be okay?"

Doctor Yates smiled then answered, "We can't keep you in Florida." He turned to my dad. "I believe we asked for your family doctor's name when you admitted Mitchell. I'll have the nurse check and send over all the information we have." The doctor turned to leave, then glanced back and said, "Take care of your mom."

Dad put his hand over mine as the doctor left the room. "You surprised me. I thought you wanted to stay."

"I want to stay in Florida and finish my work here, but it would be better for everyone if I came home. You're right. I can call Mr. O'Brien. Plus, I can't wait to see my friends and tell them all about this trip."

Mateo and Emmie came in singing *We Wish You a Merry Christmas.*

Dad laughed then asked, "Where's your dad, Mateo?"

"He's helping Violet's neighbor. He said to wish you a merry Christmas, Mitchell."

Dad walked to the doorway. "I'm going to get a cup of coffee and make some calls from the cafeteria."

Emmie took my hand and gave a squeeze. "How are you feeling?"

"I'm good but can't leave until tomorrow."

Mateo went to the opposite side of my bed. "That's too bad. We stopped to see if you could go with us."

Emmie's face flushed red. "Don't be mean, Mateo." She appeared flustered. "We're going to take an airboat ride."

My phone rang. "It's Haylee." I tapped the screen. "Haylee, I'm so glad you called."

"Merry Christmas. Andy and I are at the Goodrich farm and decided to try calling you again. I'll put you on speaker. First, tell me how you are?"

"Go ahead and put me on speaker. I put you on speaker because Mateo is here with Emmie. I'm doing much better after eating and a night's rest. How are you and Andy?"

Andy's big voice boomed, "Come home. We want to hear all about your vacation. Mateo talked to us last night. Is it true that a panther attacked you?"

Mateo and Emmie headed to the door. "Bye." That's all they said and left to have fun, which shouldn't have bothered me, but it did.

"Yes, it's true, and I'll have a scar to prove it. The doctor said that the wildcat might have thought my leg was a toy. There's a lot to tell you. I think we'll be home in a couple of days. I can't wait to see you both." We chatted for about a half-hour before my dad came back into the room, and I said goodbye to my friends. *It will be so great to see them.*

"I'm going to call mom and see how she's feeling."

Dad sat in the recliner next to the bed. "Wait a few minutes. I just talked to Miguel and asked him if a flight home tomorrow would be okay with him. Then, after calling the airline, I called your mom to tell her our flight number and to expect us late tomorrow night."

"So soon."

Dad nodded then stood at the bedside. "Do you have any idea of how proud your mother and I are of you?"

"Proud of my disastrous trip?"

"I looked at the pictures on your camera. This trip will make one heck of a story. Your mom and I are both a bit envious of you. Your life looks to be one quest after another, always chasing the story."

"I love writing and learned a lot on this little journey. Wonder what will be next?"

Dad smiled, and with a twinkle in his eye, he said, "The bank is opening a new branch near Tucson, Arizona. I'm going to help with the opening next summer after things settle down. Your mom and I heard that the air is better in Arizona for people that have breathing problems."

"You mean we might live there?" My heart sank. I never dreamed of a move so far from our family and friends.

"I guess that it would be an adventure for all of us if we moved, but no decisions have been made. I have to check it all out when I go to Tucson for the bank. Want to go with me?"

My mind whirled in a hundred directions. I had read about ghost towns around Tucson, they would be fun to explore and write about. Mom would hate the heat in Arizona, so I doubted we would move there. Maybe they would let me take a friend.

Dad's raised eyebrow indicated that he wanted to know what I was thinking.

So, I told him.

ABOUT THE AUTHOR

Sharon Willett writes to capture young peoples' imagination and get them excited about the world of books. Reading is an adventure giving an entrance into worlds that may be otherwise unreachable.

Stranded in the Everglades is the second book in the Mitchell Lavender series. Please post your review on Goodreads, Amazon, and be sure to tell your friends.

Made in the USA
Middletown, DE
07 February 2022